T0159056

The
Lotto Fix
Finale

Frank Stephens

authorHOUSE®

AuthorHouse™
1663 Liberty Drive
Bloomington, IN 47403
www.authorhouse.com
Phone: 1 (800) 839-8640

Published by AuthorHouse   11/02/2018

ISBN: 978-1-5462-6717-1 (sc)
ISBN: 978-1-5462-6716-4 (e)

Print information available on the last page.

Any people depicted in stock imagery provided by Getty Images are models,
and such images are being used for illustrative purposes only.
Certain stock imagery © Getty Images.

This book is printed on acid-free paper.

This book is dedicated to a great friend. One who spent a lot of time teaching me values and a good work ethic. More than that, a friend, who taught me many things about life. Among the things he taught me was, how to treat people with kindness and fairness. A guy, who always had my back and always encouraged me to go for my dreams, a man I always held with the highest respect. A special kind of man. Thanks Dad

Contents

Chapter 1

Sometimes the most unusual circumstances can result in the greatest of memories, and so it was with Mike. It was a dark and stormy night the first time Mike met Bill. Growing up in Florida meant you got to witness sudden storms that seemed to grow out of nowhere. This was one of those nights. It was one of those really dark and stormy afternoons due to hurricane Joseph that was getting closer to downtown Miami. Even though Mike was a long time residence of Miami and had witnessed many hurricanes, including hurricane Donna, which caused several millions of dollars worth of damage, he always took allprecautions whenever a hurricane approached. Mike had taken all of the precautions that he could take. He shut off the water, raised the air conditioner up to eighty and had given a key to his trusted secretary before heading out to meet up with his old friend Bill. Bill was one of those steady easy going guys who always seemed to be in complete control. Mike felt that wasn't the case when they had talked earlier and Bill had asked him to come to Tallahassee and wouldn't talk about it over the phone. It wasn't like Bill to be so mysterious and Mike was concerned. He made arrangements for Brenda his secretary to take care of the office while he was gone and went home and packed up a suitcase. As Mike pulled his Corvette onto Flagler Street and headed North to Lejune road he recalled the early days when he and Bill first met. Although Mike and Bill were on different police departments in Dade County, their zones overlapped. At that time Mike was a police officer with the town of Medley located just north and west of the Miami airport, and Bill was with the town of Hialeah. Although both of the towns were small and on the outskirts of Miami there seemed to be no lack of action. Hialeah and Medley were neighboring towns and the bars in Hialeah closed at one am and in Medley the bars closed at three am which meant a lot of drivers heading to Medley from Hialeah that already was if not over close to the limit and a number of times both towns worked the same area so officers from both departments usually worked together.

On any given Saturday night, there was no shortage of drivers driving impaired. In fact, it was one of those times that Mike and Bill met. They met while both were responding to a traffic accident just North of the 74th avenue exit on the Palmetto expressway. It was one of those typical afternoons when the afternoon shower had made the road a little slicker than usual. In Miami when it rains the roads are as slick as they are up North when it snows. What causes that is the accumulation of oil that drips on the road from all the cars going by and just settles on the blacktop. Then when it rains of course oil and water creates a slick condition. One of those days, when traffic although moving along at a crawl, was going well until a tractor trailer driver trying to get home in a hurry over reacted The accident occurred where both towns shared a small strip of the Palmetto expressway along with Dade County but were jurisdiction never seemed to be a problem. The accident happened just as the four o'clock traffic was building. The tractor trailer was loaded with chickens and was headed to market. It was sideswiped by a sports car. The car was driven by two young ladies who were celebrating the weekend a little bit early and lost control. The truck driver swerved to avoid a serious accident but couldn't keep the truck form tipping over and releasing about four hundred scared chickens. When Mike and Bill pulled up almost simultaneously, it appeared that four hundred imprisoned chickens had just been granted their freedom and were taking full advantage of it. There were chickens running everywhere and several people running after them trying to get them back into the cages that were left unbroken from the accident. Although it wasn't a funny incident and thank goodness no one was seriously hurt both Mike and Bill had trouble controlling their laughter when they observed all those people just running after and falling down and scooping and diving to get those chickens under control. It took them several hours to get everything straight and all the chickens rounded up. Finally they got things cleared and running smooth again.

The two young ladies got to spend the night in the local jail and got their car impounded. After working the accident, Mike and Bill went to the little diner just off the north south river drive exit to complete the paperwork. It was the end of the shift for both and by the time, they completed the paperwork they had struck up a friendship. They discovered they had several things in common including their military service. Mike had been a combat medic and Bill had served in the army air-born. Both had migrated from the north. Bill from Queens New York and Mike from a little town in Illinois. They would share a lot of good times in the upcoming years. In the years to come, this night would be one they would remember for a while as they were sitting there awaiting an approaching hurricane. As they sat and talked, they discovered they had a lot in common. Both had a love for antique automobiles and both enjoyed the same kind of music. Mike was a lover of the fifties style custom cars deemed lead sleds and Bill leaned more toward anything he could "soup up". Hurricane Jonah was heading for a direct hit to downtown Miami and it wasn't long before they found out their shifts had been extended. As the patrol cars sat driver to driver, they talked about friends and family. Both were divorced and had children that they visited when shifts would allow and in the years to follow both would share time with each other and the kids. Bill was also a banjo player who jammed on a weekly basis with a group when he had the time off. Mike on the other hand, was a rhythm guitar player who sat in with several local bands when the time allowed. It was this mutual respect and similar likes that would cement their friendship in the upcoming years.

The wind was picking up and the rain was getting heaver by the minute. The weather channel was predicting winds of one hundred sixty miles and hour which meant a long night and lots of damage. It seemed to be getting darker and darker by the minute. Hour by hour the winds got stronger and stronger and they soon reached a point where all Mike and Bill could do was hunker down and wait it out and hope for the best. They pulled their cars front to back as is the custom so that each could keep an eye on the others blind spot and make sure no one could approach from the rear of the car without the other one spotting them. Before the storm was finished there would be planes scattered across the runway on both side of the airport with one almost reaching North West Seventh Street. It would look like someone with a giant spatula came along and flipped the planes over like one would flip eggs while frying them. The wind would carry several smaller planes beyond the airport and deposit them along major streets. The trees that lined the streets would snap like twigs and roofs and debris would be scattered every-where. Many of the stores would board up their windows and doors, especially those who had been through a major hurricane or two. Those who were foolish enough to just let it ride would come back to merchandise scattered over the floors and windows shattered and water damage. The big thirty by eight foot sign that lit up the department store on north west seventh street and thirty ninth avenue, would disappear and never be seen again. One major department would suffer a major loss when the roof split right down the middle and water formed a beautiful waterfall that ran all night. It was all over there would be piles and piles of trees and debris that would line the streets for weeks to come and the cleanup and repair would take months. There would be a lot of damage to the area but luckily, only a few fatalities mostly due to thrill seekers who just wanted to experience a hurricane out on the streets. Of course there would be the usual looters that would try to take advantage of the situation and steal whatever they could get their hands on but this storm was so powerful that it discouraged even the looters. Thankfully, this night Mike and Bill didn't experience any of that phenomenon.

Mike and Bill would spend time stopping snowbirds and warning them to get to shelter. The Florida highway patrol had closed the palmetto, but there were always a few thrill seekers out there. As the winds would pick up it would become more and more dangerous with limbs and object flying through the air as missiles. It seemed like it was at least a twenty-four hour storm but in reality was only about six hours before they were able to call it a night. Mike and Bill would survive that and many more and go on to take different paths. Mike would go on to work for Metro –Dade Police department and Bill would move to Tallahassee to work for the governors' office as an investigator and personal security to the governor. Over the years, they kept in touch with at least a weekly phone call and would visit each other when vacation rolled around. They also got to spend a little time when the governor would come to Miami. Although Mike was never the high society type he blended in well at those times when he attended the governors dinners and ball. It also gave him the ability to meet some important contacts that proved in valuable to him later when he became a private detective. Although he enjoyed the department, Mike felt he could be of better service in the private arena where he could get more personally involved. As Mike headed north on Lejune road toward thirty- sixth avenue he thought to himself,

"Could that have possibly have been thirty years ago?"

"Wow" he exclaimed as he turned to get on the Palmetto heading toward the Florida turnpike. He realized it was almost thirty two years ago that he and Bill had been sharing a friendship.

They had shared lots of good times. They had lots of good memories in thirty two years. He set the cruise control at seventy and as the car purred along he remembered a few of those times he and Bill had shared over the years, Although there were a lot of great memories one in particular was the time that the President of the United States had visited his house in Key Biscayne. Key Biscayne was the area that the President would go to when he wanted to escape the Washington crowd.

That brought back a smile as Mike recalled the incident. Both had gotten to work the traffic detail along the route. Whenever the President decided to visit his Key Biscayne home, it always presented a traffic problem because the only route to the Key was one that was traveled a lot by the locals. That was because Key Biscayne was also the causeway that all the locals traveled in mass on the weekends heading to the beaches and picnic areas. In addition to being, an area where one could launch a boat the area also boasted a zoo, a roller skating area and lots of benches for a family to have a picnic. Although one could stop any-where along the causeway to go swimming, the best area was at the end of the park. Beyond the swimming area and towards the end of the causeway was the area where the elite build their resort homes. These were homes that show business personalities and major business people had weekend getaways built. These were the places the rich and famous went to when they wanted to get away from it all. It was an area that was heavily patrolled. This was one of those weekends where everyone had decided to go to the beach and the President had decided likewise. The cars were at a virtual standstill and the heat made a few tempers flare. Lucky that most of the locals were used to the traffic jams that were created and kept their tempers in check. As he cruised along he recalled how right in the middle of the president getting ready to land at Homestead Air Force Base that time the base was turned into a tizzy. Seemed at the same time the Presidents plane was approaching the air base a small plane was spotted on radar also trying to land. The tower kept trying to reach the pilot of the seemingly small plane to no avail. Try as they may there was no answer from the pilot of the small plane. It was only after the Presidents plane had landed and the other plane landed right behind him that the tower discovered it was a Russian MIG with a defecting Cuban pilot. The pilot had sneaked in under the radar and the tower didn't seem to be aware of it. This incident became a leading story in the national newspapers for quite a while. It probably caused a bunch of rule changes along with some tactic changes.

The tower kept trying to wave the pilot off to no avail because the pilot was running out of fuel and didn't understand English, He saw a runway and he put the Mig down. By the time, they realized it was a Russian jet it had already landed on one of the runaways and the secret service had swarmed over the poor unsuspecting pilot. A warning had gone out to stop all the air traffic and divert it to another route. However, this pilot wasn't on the same frequency and landed. Made the secret service realize how vulnerable they were and I'm sure that landing led to a great number of rule changes and the way the military protected the Florida Coast.

As he drove on, he remembered more of the times they had shared. One of the better ones was the times they shared at the Venetian pool in Coral Gables with the kids. The Venetian pool sat in the middle of the old Coral Gables area. It was a man-made pool that featured a sandy beach area as well as a giant pool with man-made caves that one could go into. They weren't very deep but were made shallow so even kids go into them. There were also cliffs that one could dive off of if one was brave enough. Although they were only about fifteen feet high they were still a thrill. It was a man-made area that presented an alternative to fighting the traffic heading to the beaches each weekend. The streets leading up to the pool from southwest eight were lined up with magnificent trees that formed an overhang along the route. The trees became a victim of the storm that year and left a bare looking street that altered the appearance of the area. As he drove along he marveled just how much he and Bill had in common. They both liked to play and listen to music and would enjoy the music at Mother's lounge on Southwest Eight street, or the country lounge called the Silver Spur lounge on Fifty-Seventh Avenue. They also liked to go to the Hideaway lounge where a local country singer did a great act. Funny thing was neither one drank. In fact, both were famous for their club soda with a twist of lemon drink. Overall, they had shared some good times and some sad times. They also shared some fun times, like at one of their scuba diving excursions. Mike and Bill liked to scuba dive off the beach in nearby Hollywood but to do so they had to go out Government cut. Now at the time

Bill owned a thirteen and a halve tri hull boat that was just about big enough to carry the gear and the two of them. One of the officers that worked with Bill named Frank found out about their scuba adventures and asked to go along. Although the tri hull was barely big enough for two, they both agreed to let him come along. The day came for the dive and this officer showed up with a cheap kid store mask and fins. They were a little reluctant to allow him but he begged and they finally relented. Because it was Franks first time they decided to keep the dive confined to a shallow depth of around thirty feet.

They gave Frank a quick crash course on how to clear your mask if it fills up with water while under water and how to keep track of your air by keeping an eye on the gauges. They went over the equipment on the shore before heading out to the ocean and all seemed ok until they got out in the ocean. It was one of those perfect days for diving. The ocean was calm and the morning was warm with just a little sea breeze. Going out so-called government cut was a chore in itself. Although while in the cut itself the water was calm one had to put up with those thirty-five foot speedboats that created a wake for the fifteen-foot tri-hull they were in. Once outside the government cut the waters turned a clear blue and the seas ere calm with only a foot or less swell. They went south of the cut about a halve a mile and cut the engine. After they cut the motor and dropped an anchor to secure their spot, they rechecked their tanks, put them on and motioned for Frank to do the same. The motioned for Frank to go backwards over the side but when they dropped anchor a pair of dolphins arrived and Frank saw the fins, got a little scared and wouldn't go in. Mike and Bill both tried to explain that as long as the dolphins were around the sharks more than likely would stay away but Frank wasn't buying it till Mike and Bill went in and showed him it was ok. Frank jumped in and promptly started to sink to the bottom like a rock. The bottom was about thirty feet at that point but the cheap mask he had bought started to leak due to his mustache which didn't allow the proper seal. By this time they were about twenty feet deep and Bill kept trying to show Frank how to clear his mask by tipping it up and letting the air bubbles from the tank blow out the water, but Frank kept shaking his head no like he was afraid to try it. Over and over Bill filled his mask with water on purpose and showed Frank how to clear it and over and over Frank shook his head no. Of course, all the while they were under water and sinking lower. They reached about thirty feet and with a sad puppy dog look on his face Frank pulled the chord on the emergency vest that divers wear and shot up to the top like a ball that has just been released under water. It was all Mike and Bill could do to keep from busting out with laughter under water as they swam up to the boat. Needless to say, that was Frank's first and last try at scuba diving. Mike chuckled as he drove along and recalled the incident.

Even though Bill was still in Tallahassee, he and Mike kept in touch every Sunday and shot the bull about old times. They would spend about an hour on the phone going over the past week's events and close with a talk at you next week.

Bill had recently retired from the governors' security detail but Mike was still plugging away as a private detective.

Mike had retired from Metro Dade when he turned 52

and even though he had a nice pension he missed the feeling of satisfaction he had gotten putting the bad guys in jail and helping those who needed it.

Being a private detective had gotten him involved in a few big cases and being a private detective he was able to use a few, shall we say, more creative methods to help his old buddies to get the evidence on the bad guys, and they in return did Mike a favor now and then. Mike had a little office around the corner from 39th avenue and Flagler Street that served his purpose. It was a small office but did what he wanted. It had just enough room for his office, and a little reception area for his long time friend Brenda Lee. Mike had met Brenda when he was on the force and she worked dispatch. She was a petite middle age woman who knew how to handle any situation and who was extremely dependable. Brenda was single and wanted it that way. Just the kind of woman Mike wanted in his office. With BL, as Mike called her, watching the office Mike could feel free to pursue any case he needed to knowing the home front was covered. Being retired he could afford to take only the cases he felt were important and not take every one that came along. Over the years Mike and Brenda had become friends and were able to share problems and dinners together without any pressure from anyone to advance the relationship. They also shared a mutual respect for each other so it made for a great professional relationship and made the office run smooth.

Mike was getting close to that 60 year old mark, which meant a few more hours in the gym pumping iron and a little more cardio work to maintain his 6foot 2inch two hundred pound frame. Mike worked out four days a week and played racket ball to stay in shape. Although Mike was a private investigator his retirement status gave him access to the police range, and he would take the small arms classes offered by several retired officers and utilize the sources available to him. In addition, having a concealed weapon permit meant spending a few days a month on the shooting range. It also kept him in touch with the guys still on the force. It served two purposes. One the new guys coming on would get to know him from the veterans and two they knew it was a quid pro quo relationship. If they needed help with a case he was there for them and he sometimes would get a helping hand on a case he was working on.

Chapter 2

He eased the Corvette onto the Florida turnpike and kicked her up to seventy five. The throaty sound of the 383 stroker motor he had installed the year before rumbling through the flow-master mufflers made an almost musical sound as he headed North. It was one of those beautiful early mornings that made Mike glad he had a corvette with t-tops. He had taken them off as he started off. As the sun glistened off the gold pearl cinnabar paint of the Vette he headed up the Florida turnpike. He kicked back and enjoyed the view of the sky and the sound of the motor while listening to some oldies music by the Legends of Doo Wop who were personal friends of his. Five hours later, he eased the corvette onto I-75 and decided to stop off for a while and kill two stones with one bird and visit his old drag racing buddy John who was operating a museum just south of Ocala. The museum was filled with several of the cars john had raced and achieved many awards with like the first one to go faster than two hundred miles an hour in the quarter mile and it even held the dragster he clocked over three hundred miles an hour in.

In addition John had collected many antique automobiles and those were on display there. One of Mike's favorite cars was the Mercury that was in the series Happy Days and belonged to Fonzie. It was one of those all day museums that one could go and almost feel the excitement of drag racing. John was a world class dragster driver and still held many records for drag racing. In fact he had recently just set the world record for an electric dragster. Even though he was a bit older than Mike he was still active in his shop and still active in chasing the two hundred miles per hour quarter mile record in an electric dragster, There was no one who had more knowledge of old cars and knew how to fix them than John and even at this time John was still building dragsters and hot rods. No matter now famous he had gotten John never forgot his early days when he had live further south and struggled with the kids. In fact till this day John hosts a Toys for Kids show every December at his museum sponsored by a local classic car club called the Twilight Cruisers.

Mike had attended one of those shows complete with the local sheriffs K-9 and swat team and great old time music played by a disc jockey. He noted that a local charity gained over ten thousand dollars' worth of toys for underprivileged kids and this had been going on for over fifteen years. While attending that show Mike marveled at how many classics, antique, hot rods and custom cars attended that show. There were over four hundred cars with several species that he didn't realize still existed. One was a combination car and boat that one could drive from the road right into the lake and back out again. There was an old time milk truck that was the norm in the forties. The one where the milk was delivered every day in glass bottles on a daily basis. In those days the crème would rise to the top of the bottle and in the winter up north would sometimes freeze and pop the top of the milk bottle. There were several more outstanding cars like a 68 Firebird convertible that had been completely restored and a yellow thirty ford coupe like the one in the movie American Graffiti. Many years ago Mike had met John when both were drag racing at the old Amelia Earhardt airfield in Miami near Opa-Locka. It was almost like a make-shift racing strip, with a major roadway at one end and a major roadway at the completed side of the strip. At the far end of the strip Lejune road went smack across the end of the emergency stopping area and sometimes presented a scary ride, especially if your brakes failed. Several times that had happened. You did however get to scare the motorists heading North on Lejune road. Because of the small stopping area the track used to keep a person out on the roadway in case the drag cars were coming across to try to wave off the drivers. Fortunately there was never a major incident in which anyone got seriously hurt.

As he pulled off the interstate, Mike eased the corvette into the Sleep-Ease hotel he marveled at the changes that had taken place it the area since he had last visited. What used to be just a little gas stop off on the interstate was now a busy area with several hotels and restaurants filling out the landscape. Although it had grown, a lot the area still remained a rural area charm with some big horse farms located just a half of mile away from the exit. It would be good to see his old friend. He called John, who happily agreed to meet him at one of the restaurants. It wasn't long before john walked into the restaurant and as they greeted each other Mike marveled at the condition John was in. John was about five foot ten and built like a professional athlete. Mike noticed that john was sporting a new beard that he kept neatly trimmed. "How in the world do you stay in such great shape?" asked Mike. "It seems to be getting harder every year." Said John "but I've taken up bike riding and it has made a world of difference. They sat down, ordered dinner, and shared a few old memories.

"Do you remember the first time we met John?" asked Mike.

"Near as I can recall wasn't it at the old Amelia Earhart airfield dragstrip?"

"Yes it was, and I had a Kaiser with a performance Olds J-2 motor in it and you were running a D-altered dragster."

The drag strip had no idea what class to run Mike in so the pitted him in an exhibition race against John. As they sat in the restaurant, telling the story John asked Mike what happened in the race.

"Well John" Mike said.

"When the Christmas tree blinked green I pulled the nicest whole shot you ever saw. Unfortunately you were already heading down the track and thought me what it means to have your doors blown off". They both laughed and enjoyed the memories.

"So what brings you up this way Mike?" John asked.

"Got a distress call from an old friend of mine that said it was important and so here I am on my way to Tallahassee."

They sat for a little while longer and both agreed not to let the time slip away from them before the next visit. Mike went on to the hotel to catch some sleep so he could get an early start the next morning.

The next morning was one of those perfect mornings. There was relative low humidity and the temperature reading around 58 degrees. It would take about six hours or so to make Tallahassee so Mike grabbed a coffee and a breakfast sandwich to go, hopped into the corvette and eased onto I-75. He wondered why Bill had been so secretive on the phone when he asked Mike to please come up to Tallahassee and help him with a problem. As he drove the highway, he thought that it was sure out of character for Bill to ask for his help. Bill was the kind of soft spoken, laid back guy who never asked for help but handled everything himself. Bill was the kind of slow, but steady friend that you could always count on. Mike knew when he got the mysterious phone call that it must be something serious; otherwise, Bill would have handled whatever it was that was bothering him by himself. As he drove along he kept glancing at the rear view mirror and thought he kept seeing a SUV behind him but reasoned that he wasn't the only one going somewhere and they might just be heading in the same direction. He made a mental note to keep an eye on the SUV and see if it was following him. Mike turned on the radio popped in a cd and adjusted the cruise control. His love of music covered many genre's. All the way from his favorite Roy Orbison of the fifty's and sixty's to Andre Bochelli. The nice thing about the cd's is that Mike could mix the music and enjoy the tunes while he drove. Mike eased back in his seat, turned up the volume on the radio and kept time with the tunes. About an hour and a half later, he approached the Interstate ten interchange.

As he turned onto I-10 heading west, Mike had that uneasy feeling that someone was still following him. He pulled into the rest stop, headed for the rest rooms and then turned back to see if he could see that SUV he had spotted in the rear view mirror. Sure enough it had pulled in one of the spots about half way down the rest stop but there didn't seem to be anyone sitting in it. He walked around the corvette and suddenly got back into the corvette and pulled back onto I-10. The speedometer quickly hit 100 and Mike kept it there for a minute to throw off anybody that might be following him. He then pulled off the first exit and pulled under the bridge for a few minutes till he heard the SUV traveling at high speed go whizzing by. He waited a few minutes then headed back up on I-10. He kept glancing at the rear view mirror but never saw anything more of the SUV. A few hours later he turned off I-10 onto Thomasville road heading south and pulled into the Hilton Garden Inn, which was, he hoped, close to his old friend.

Mike put in a call to his old friend Bill, left a message and waited for his call in the coffee shop next to the hotel. It wasn't long before Mike recognized the broad shoulders and walk that was Bills coming through the door. Seemed like Bills head, like Mikes, head had grown faster than their hair, for both were noticeably losing the follicle challenge. .

Bill still had that bounce in his step when he walked. He always looked like he was dancing when he walked. It was one of those habits that got him a lot of kidding from his pears. They used to call him The Gene Kelly of the force. After greeting each other, they ordered up something to eat. They talked a little about old times and after a short time started to tell Mike why he called and requested help from his old friend.

"Mike, we've know each other a long time and have been through a lot of things together. You know I wouldn't ask you to come up here if I didn't think it was crucial. It was while I was on my last detail with the governor when I was in the men's room at the ballroom here in the Hilton and overheard a conversation between two people that made me jump out of my shoes"

"Jump out of your shoes? That doesn't sound like the guy I shared all those times and situations over the years with."

"I know Mike but this seems to be much bigger that anything we ever encountered all those years we were on the force. In fact if I hadn't heard it with my own ears I would have though I was listening to a movie plot."

"What did you hear Bill and who was it?"

"I tried to look out the door and make them out but I never saw them before. They were dressed in tuxedos and looked like everyone else there I don't know who they were but they were discussing what to do with the next months lotto money."

"Next month? Hell Bill this week's winner hasn't even been announced yet, how could they know who was going to win next months?"

"I know Mike. That's what struck me funny too. I was trying to think of how anyone could possibly fix that. Listen let's go over to my place and I'll tell you what I know and we can come up with a battle plan."

"Sounds like a plan old buddy; you still live in that same apartment?"

"Yes I'm still at the same place Mike."

They went outside where Bill had brought his big old sedan. Bill had bought that old sedan years ago and although it was now reaching antique status it was still in great shape. Bill had just gotten it painted and a new engine put in it and it ran and looked like new. Mike got into the sedan and Bill was just about to get into the drivers' side when a dark blue SUV came around the corner, struck the drivers' door and knocked Bill up into the air. He landed on the hood of the old sedan and rolled off to the front. By this time Mike had gotten out of his side came around the front of the car and had pulled out his trusty old 38 Super automatic and fired several shots in the direction of the SUV that had hit Bill and sped off.

Mike grabbed his cell phone out of his pocket and quickly dialed 911. "I need an ambulance outside the Hilton Garden Inn on Thomasville road and hurry."

He leaned over his old friend and checked to see if he was still breathing, which he was but Mike could tell he was in serious shape. His body looked like it had been drug over sandpaper with lacerations all over. His shirt had been ripped off and one of his shoes was missing. There was blood coming from under his shirt and he had a big knot on his forehead, which looked to be growing bigger every second. By this time there was a crowd that had come out of the hotel restaurant and several people had come running out of the hotel and one of them brought a blanket, which Mike used to cover Bill to try to keep him warm. He bent down and leaned over his old friend and said,

"Hang in there old buddy the ambulance is on the way." Bill seemed like he was trying to say something so Mike leaned over him and heard Bill whisper

"The book, save the book". Then Bill closed his eyes and Mike shook him.

"Stay with me buddy you're going to make it, just hang in there. Don't quit now you still owe me a dinner." That seemed to bring Bill back around.

Although it was only a matter of minutes, to Mike it seemed like an hour went by before the rescue squad and EMT's arrived. Before the EMT's could get out a patrol car came screaming in behind. The patrol car slid up behind the rescue squad and before it could come to a complete stop two of Tallahassee's finest got out and approached Mike with weapons drawn and ordered Mike to drop the weapon and get on the ground face down with his arms out, palms up.

"Easy boys" Mike said. I'm a private investigator up from Miami and this is my long time friend. We both served on Metro Dade for years"

"If you give me a chance I have my identification here in my wallet."

"Do it slowly and with only two fingers" stated the officers.

Mike slowly reached into his coat pocket and pulled out his ID card and his shield that he carried. The officers holstered their weapons and started to talk to Mike about the accident.

"How did the accident occur? One of the officers asked.

"That was no accident" Mike said.

"Whoever it was, deliberately tried to kill my friend and I need to get to the hospital"

The officers took the information where Mike was staying and told him they would give him a ride to the hospital. He got into the back of the squad car and they headed over to Tallahassee Memorial Hospital on Miccosukee Rd. It seemed like an eternity before they arrived at the hospital but in reality, it was only a few minutes. As they pulled up to the emergency entrance Mike was met by two detectives. Mike got out and was headed in to find his friend when the doctor stopped him and said.

"Take your time, he's in surgery and will be there for a while"

"You can wait in there." She pointed to a waiting room just across from the emergency entrance.

Mike went into the waiting room followed by two detectives. They introduced themselves.

"Hi I'm Joe Thomas" the younger of the two said.

"Hey I'm Wayne Kaminski" said the other detective.

"We're with the Sheriffs dept and we're investigating the hit and run".

They seemed like a miss match pair, because Joe was a about five foot five and built solid and Mike noticed his hands looked like those of a boxer and showed he wasn't afraid of physical work and Wayne appeared to be about five foot seven and a little on the slim side. Joe presented himself as friendly while Wayne seemed to be smarter than everyone type. Something about Wayne that made Mike feel a little uneasy like he was not the most trusting one of the pair. Mike just shrugged that off to the years in his type of work and old habits.

"I worked with a Bob Thomas at Metro Dade in Miami" Mike said.

"Is he any relationship to you?"

"That was my uncle," Joe said.

"He was on the motorcycle brigade for years until he

reached the age that he had to retire. He worked his way up to captain just before he left."

"As I recall he was one of the good guys and received quite a few commendations form the department. In fact I think he was the one who saved several people in an accident on the Palmetto." Mike said.

"Sounds like you two need to spend some time reminiscing, but how about we make it some other time." Wayne said.

Mike thought of saying something but thought it can wait. He wondered why Wayne was acting so gruff with a fellow former officer but reasoned that many times a police officer doesn't really respect a private detective for a number of reasons and brushed it off.

"Now that were all acquainted and cozy tell us what's this all about? Asked Wayne

"I don't know" said Mike " Bill and I worked together in Miami and he called me up with a sense of urgency and wanted to talk about something important that he wouldn't talk about over the phone, so I came up to meet him. We were going to grab a bite to eat when that SUV came out of the shadows and ran right into Bill"

"You mean you came all the way up here and he didn't give you any hint of what he wanted. Not a clue or persons name or anything?" Wayne said.

Joe could see Mike was getting a little irritated so he stepped in between Mike and Wayne and said,

"Sounds like you don't think it was an accident Mike." "That was definitely not an accident. He came right at us at high speed, never swerved or slowed down at all. He never even tried to miss him. That was definitely on purpose." said Mike.

Do you have any idea why someone would want to kill Bill" asked Wayne?

"Not a clue yet, but I will, you can take that to the bank. Mike said. "Mike did you happen to catch a tag number?" Joe asked.

"No it happened so fast while I was in the car I didn't get a chance to catch anything but the color which was a dark blue or black."

"OK," said Joe. "We will try to see if any of the traffic cams or witness saw anything and let you know."

"Remember Mike you are not in Miami now, so step lightly and let us do our job." Wayne said. "Stay available to us and don't leave town.

"We'll keep you advised if we find out anything Mike." Wayne said as he and Joe turned and started to leave the area. They were going to go back and start a canvas of the area where the crime scene investigators were now gathering evidence.

"Where are you staying Mike?" Joe asked.

"I'm at the Hampton on Thomas Rd." said Mike.

"But I'll be here at the hospital until I hear what's going on with Bill."

"How about giving me a ride back so I can get my car"?

On the way back to the car Joe and Wayne asked again if he had any idea why Bill would call him and ask him to come to Tallahassee.

"We never got that far, we were just catching up to old times when we were heading over to his apartment but whatever it was it must be big". Mike said.

Wayne kept asking Mike about what Bill had said.

"Did he say anything that would give us a clue? Did he mention any names? De he say he knew who was behind all this?"

Mike kept answering no to each of his questions and was getting a little annoyed at the constant barrage of questions. Finally, they arrived back at the coffee shop. Once again Wayne reminded him to stay available.

Mike got into the Corvette, started up the powerful beast, and headed over to the Tallahassee Memorial hospital. He pulled into the emergency parking area, parked the Corvette, and entered the emergency area of the hospital. He stopped at the desk to ask where Bill was. The girl behind the glass enclosed counter told him to wait a minute and someone would be right with him. It seemed like a couple of hours but in reality it was only a short time later when an attendant wearing a set of green scrubs approached Mike and said "Your friend is still in surgery right now. You can wait for him upstairs in the surgery waiting room."

Mike went upstairs, grabbed a cup of coffee and went over in his mind the conversation that had taken place between him and Bill a few days prior.

Bill wasn't the type to panic at anything and Mike had seen him handle plenty of dangerous situations coolly and calmly but when they talked, Mike had noticed there seemed to be a urgency in Bills voice. Mike recalled a piece of the conversation and wondered what Bill meant when he said "The book, save the book." after he had gotten hit by the van.

Chapter 3

It seemed like days had passed but in reality it was about four hours later when a man came in wearing the familiar hospital scrubs and approached Mike.

"Hi I'm Dr Zeph. Your friend is injured pretty badly but he'll pull through ok although he will be sedated for a few days while his body recovers." We have him on a medically induced coma, He has four broken ribs and a concussion but he will be OK."

"Can I see him?" Mike asked.

"Yes but only for a short moment. The more time he has the more his body has time to recover." said the doctor.

The nurse was adjusting the breathing machines and monitors when Mike walked into the room where they had taken Bill.

Bill looked pretty bad. His head was bandaged and there was a cast on his left arm and cuts and bruises everywhere.

Mike put his hand on Bills shoulder and said,

"It's going to be all right partner. You just get better and leave the rest to me."

He sat there for about an hour and tried to figure out how in the world could someone rig the lotto and if they did it must be a hell of a big operation. He finally felt that Bill was in good hands and that he could do better trying to find out who put his old buddy in this position. Mike left the hospital and headed over to the Capital Ridge Apartments where Bill had a town house apartment. It was in an upscale neighborhood that seemed to be quiet and filled with professional people. He gathered that from all of the fairly new cars sitting in the parking places. He walked inside and found the managers apartment. He rang the doorbell and a thin older gentleman answered.

"Can I help you? He asked.

"I hope so." Mike replied.

Mike talked to the manager and told him what had happened to Bill and after a while he agreed to let Mike into the apartment but only after he showed him his credentials and a picture of him and Bill on the force back in Miami that he had in his wallet.

The landlord opened the door and Mike immediately pushed him aside and drew his trusty Colt Super auto from his holster. The apartment looked like a miniature tornado had snuck in and rearranged the apartment. There were books and lamps just scattered around the apartment. The couch upholstery had been cut. Some pictures that were on the wall had been taken down the backs cut open and then thrown to the ground and all the kitchen cabinets had been opened and several boxes of cereal had been cut and thrown down on the floor and even the rug had been pulled up in spots. Mike motioned the manager to stay put while he cleared the apartment. Slowly and systematically, Mike went from room to room checking for anyone who might still be there. He was careful not to touch anything or disturb anything.

"Holy cow what the heck happened here?" the landlord said.

"What the heck were they looking for?"

"I don't know but they sure went to a lot of trouble trying to find it so it must be damn important."

Mike made sure the apartment was clear to enter and then asked the landlord to hold off for a while before he notified the police to give him a little time to figure this out.

"I wouldn't normally do that Mike but I think you are right this isn't a normal burglary. Just let me know when you want me to report it" said the manager.

Mike carefully looked around the apartment searching for a clue as to what someone was looking for, but couldn't see anything that might lead him to getting closer to the reason why someone would go to this kind of destruction. Clearly Bill had something somebody wanted bad enough to kill Bill and cause this much damage to Bills little two bedroom apartment. The way things looked though it didn't appear that they found what they were looking for. For a moment Mike surveyed the damage. Every dresser drawer had been pulled out and emptied and thrown on the ground. All the clothes had been pulled out of the closets and thrown on the floor. The shelves that once held boxes of memories had been pulled out of the closet and emptied on the floor.

Also in the kitchen dishes had been pulled out of their cabinets and the pots and pans were scattered on the floor. Even the bottom drawer of the oven had been pulled out and emptied. They had even emptied out the freezer. Frozen food was scattered all over the kitchen floor. In the living room all the books had been pulled off the bookshelves as though someone was looking into each page for a list of some kind. Whoever had ransacked the apartment appeared to get extremely angry and didn't appear to have found what they were looking for. As he stood there in silence Mike could hear the distant wail of the sirens.

The landlord had notified police by this time and it wasn't long before the two detectives that were assigned to Bills case pulled up.

Wayne and Joe the two detectives Mike had met at the hospital approached Mike rather quickly and Joe said

"Looks like this someone had more than a little beef with Bill"

"Yes this is beginning to look a lot more than a simple assault" said Wayne.

"What do you think your friend was into that might have led to this?" asked Wayne. "Was your friend into drugs or gambling or maybe he was attracted to the wrong lady friend"?

Joe could see that Mike was getting a little iriatated with Wayne's suggestions so he stepped in and asked Mike.

"You got any idea what they were looking for?"

"Not a clue." said Mike, "But whatever it was it sure must be important."

"Important enough to kill Bill for and I don't take it very lightly when someone tries to kill a friend of mine. Somehow they will have to answer to me."

"Listen Mike, this might just be a revenge thing. Someone

may just be trying to get even with Bill for something stupid. There are a lot of crazies out there. Let us do our job and we will keep you in the loop and when we find who is responsible for this we will let you know. "Said Joe.

"In the meantime you need to wait outside and don't disturb anything and let CSI gather any evidence they can."

The forensic team had arrived and was already hard at work dusting and bagging things and taking pictures of the scene from all angles for future evidence.

"Going back to the hotel Mike?" asked Joe.

"Think I'll stay here tonight and when the team finishes, clean up a little and try to make some sense of this." said Mike.

"We'll be finished in about thirty minutes." said a member of the CSI team.

"Think I'll go up the street and pick up a few things." Said Mike "I'll be back in a few minutes."

Mike walked up the street to a grocery store and bought some eggs, coffee, bread and fresh fruit. When he had returned back to the apartment the forensic team was finishing and packing up.

Mike started to straighten things up a bit while trying to make sense of what Bill could have possibly have gotten into to warrant this kind of destruction.

Mike knew that Bill was the kind of easy going guy that wouldn't hurt anybody unless it was absolutely necessary and then he could be your worst enemy. He also knew that Bill was the kind of a guy that you knew would never cross the line and one that you could count on. If you needed him he would be there just like Mike was here now.

After straightening up for a while he made a pot of coffee scrambled some egg whites made some toast and kicked back in Bills easy chair. It wasn't long before he had dozed off. It was about two am when Mike was awakened by the phone, He picked it up but there was no answer and after a few seconds whoever had called had hung up.

Mike pushed the star 69 button but the number came back blocked and private.

Unable to get back to sleep Mike decided to drive over to the Tallahassee Memorial hospital on Miccasuka road where Bill was and to see if there was any change to Bills condition. Bills room was in room 409 on the fourth floor and when Mike stepped off the elevator he noticed there was no guard near the room that Bill was in. There was a uneasy feeling about the area, like something was missing. It was an eerie feeling. Mike looked around but didn't see anybody. He looked down the hall but it was silent. There didn't seem to be a nurse in sight or at the nurses' station so Mike started down the hall towards the room Bill was in.

He turned the corner and entered the room. There appeared to be an orderly standing over Bill. Mike noticed that the orderly was getting ready to put a syringe into the intravenous tube attached to Bills arm.

"Hey what are you doing?" Mike asked.

The man that was dressed up as an orderly reached behind him for something but by this time Mike had crossed the room and had grabbed the man's arms.

They tumbled on to the floor and the man got in a good punch to Mikes jaw which only seemed to heighten Mikes anger. They both got up and Mike hit the guy who tumbled across the floor and knocked over the tray that was alongside Bills bed.

He rolled around and then came up off the floor with a snub nose revolver in his hand but by this time Mike had the trusty thirty eight super out of his holster and fired one shot. That shot hit the orderly in the chest and knocked him back towards the fourth story window. The glass shattered like it had been hit by a bomb and the man flew out and landed onto the ground four stories below.

Mike went over to the window to see the security guard that had been in the lobby come out and check the man for a pulse. He shook his head up at Mike. Mikes bullet had gone right through the heart killing the orderly instantly.

By this time more nurses had arrived and were in the process of checking on Bill.

Mike after making sure Bill was all right rushed down stairs to check on the body. As he came out of the lobby he noticed a dark SUV pulling away from the hospital.

He went over to the spot where he had seen the body laying on the concrete, but the body was gone. All that remained was a pool of blood and some tire tracks. It was about this time that Joe and Wayne pulled up in their unmarked car and jumped out.

"What's happened Mike?" Joe asked.

Mike explained what had happened including the fact the man was trying to inject something into Bills intravenous tube.

"What happened to the body then?" Wayne asked.

"I don't know." Mike said. "It was here when I looked out the window. Ask the guard, he heard the shot and ran out from the lobby and checked the guy for a pulse. He looked up at me and shook his head motioning that he was dead."

Body's don't just get up and leave Mike" said Wayne.

"Are you sure he was dead?

Mike was getting annoyed at the way Wayne was questioning him but Joe intervened and asked,

"What happened to the guard that we left at Bills door?"

"I didn't see any guard when I was there." Mike said.

They went upstairs to Bills room. There were doctors and nurses in the room by now and one of the nurses came over and told Mike that they didn't see the nurse assigned to that floor any-where. Wayne and Joe both drew their guns and start to check every room on the floor with Mike trailing behind them. They thought of telling him to stay put but both knew that wasn't going to happen so they cautioned him to stay behind them, Slowly they went into each room taking caution to check out each one including the bathrooms but not disturb any patients. At the end of the hall was the supply room where they kept all of the supplies. On the floor close to the door they noticed a small dripping of blood. Slowly they opened the room with guns drawn. The supply room was a converted bed room with shelves running down the middle of the room and shelves also lined both sides. They could hear what appeared to be a moaning sound coming from behind the row of shelves. They approached slowly and they found the floor nurse and the guard both shot, but alive. The uniform officer also had a nasty gash in his head where he had fallen and was just regaining conscientiousness.

"What happened?" Joe asked the officer.

"This nurse and an orderly approached me while I was

standing near the room and said they had to give him his hourly shot and the next thing I know someone hit me in the back of the head and here I am."

"Can you give us a description of the nurse?" Joe asks the officer.

"Well near as I can remember she was short, a little over five feet I would say and had dark short black hair with deep blue eyes."

"You pretty sure about that?" Joe asked.

"Yes, I remember those eyes because they were the darkest blue I have seen. Sorry I can't be of any more help".

He then lapses back into unconsciousness. By now, several nurses had arrived and were trying to attend to the nurse that had been knocked out.

Joe shouts out,

"Get a doctor here and fast."

The doctor arrives and he shouts out to the orderlies

"Get this man into surgery fast!".

As they were wheeling him away Mike said to Joe,

"We need to get CSI here to check that room over good.

They moved Bill across the hall and cordoned the room off with some crime scene tape.

The C.S.I. crew arrived shortly afterward and after checking the room for a few minutes discovered a small vial under the bed. They tagged the vial and put it in an evidence bag and said to Wayne

"We're almost done and it looks like the only major thing we have found so far was this vial." Wayne took the package looked at it and said

"Maybe we can get some prints off it."

Just then Mike arrived back in the room.

"Find anything?" he asked "Just this vial" said Joe. "But we don't know if it's part of this or not. The lab boys will give us a call as soon as they have something."

"What about the syringe and needle" Mike asked.

"What syringe and needle?" Joe asked.

"When I came into the room that guy I shot had a needle and syringe and was getting ready to put something in Bills I.V." They start to look around a little more. They look under the bed and on the bed and are just about ready to give up when one of the CSI crew pulled back the curtain and sticking in the wall was a small syringe.

"Here it is." said one of the one of the crime scene techs. He then tagged the syringe and sealed it in an evidence bag.

About that time, the doctor who was attending the nurse came into the room and said "She just had a small flesh wound and was going to be all right.

"Can we talk to her?" asked Joe.

"Yes but only for a few moments. She has a nasty bump on her head and may have received a concussion."

They go into the small cubical where the nurse is sitting up and ask. "What happened?'

"I was at the nurse's station when the orderly approached me and said he had a doctor's order to give the patient a shot. I told him that there wasn't any order on the chart for a shot and that I would need a doctor's written permission before I could allow him to give the patient a shot. That was when he pulled out the gun and hit me over the head and dragged me into the room."

"Had you ever seen him before? Do you know who he is?"

"Never saw him before and don't have a clue as to who he is." said the nurse.

"How about the nurse that was with the orderly/" asked Joe.

"I haven't seen her here before, but there must be a hundred nurses I haven't seen. She seemed different though."

"How do you mean, different? " asked Joe.

"Well she just didn't seem to be a medical person, I don't know. She just struck me as someone who would be involved with big business or the government or something like that. She just didn't fit. She looked like a nurse and acted like one but I just had an odd feeling about her. She was wearing some type of necklace, and I don't see nurses wearing jewelry on the job.'

"OK that's enough. She needs to rest now" said the doctor.

They go back out of the room and turn to Mike.

"We're going back to the station." Joe and Wayne said. "We'll catch up with you later. We'll ask the captain to post a guard around the clock here and secure this area."

"Think I'll hang around here for a while." Mike said and went into the room to sit with his old friend.

Bill looked peaceful but pale and as Mike looked at the oxygen tube on his friend, along with the intravenous tube attached to his arm, and the monitoring machine that beeped every so often, keeping a record of Bills pulse, blood pressure and breathing. He vowed to make whoever was responsible for this to pay up for it and make sure they never do it again. By now, the clock on the hospital room wall was sitting at 4AM and the two uniformed officers that Joe and Wayne had requested arrived at the scene.

Mike check their credentials and after satisfying himself he decided to return to Bills apartment to straighten up a little and catch a cat nap.

Mike arrived back at Bills and started to straighten up a little bit and after about a half hour he decided to grab a nap and finish up later. Later turned out to be noon and when Mike got up he started in the kitchen and put on some coffee.

He straightened up the apartment in a couple of hours and decided that lunch was in order.

Chapter 4

He walked out of the apartment and noticed a small diner up the street. He walked up the block and went in to sit in one of the booths and smiled at the waitress.

This was one of those 50's or 60's diners with the black and with checkered tiles, the pictures of old cars and movie stars on the walls and the replica juke boxes in each booth.

Of course now the juke box played cd's instead of 45's and the price was a dollar for two plays instead of three plays for a quarter, but it had a clearer sound than the original sound of the forty five rpm records.

The waitress came over and Mike noticed her name tag said Belinda. She was probably in her late fifties but looked like she had taken good care of herself. She had blond hair, green eyes and stood about five foot three and weighed in at about one hundred and twenty pounds was Mikes guess.

"Can I get you something to drink?" Belinda asked?

"Coffee please and if possible, and I'll take an egg white omelet with peppers, onions, tomatoes and rye toast."

"I don't believe I have ever seen a necklace quite like

Frank Stephens

that." Mike said noticing that Belinda had what looked like a necklace with a tiny Raven on it.

"It was a gift from an old friend." Belinda said.

She went away and Mike sat and reminisced back to the days when he and Bill were partners.

Bill was always on Mikes' case for eating badly and finally trained Mike to eat healthy like he did. In fact, this was Bills favorite breakfast.

The waitress returned with the coffee and said "I haven't seen you around here before."

"That's because it's my first time here." said Mike. "I came up here from Miami to help a friend."

"That must be some friend, said Belinda. "That's a long way back to Miami."

"Well, it's a short distance to travel for this guy." Mike said.

"If I had to go cross country I would do it."

"Wow you must know this friend pretty good."

"We were both on the police department and although it seems like yesterday, it was back a few years and we've been best friends ever since. We kind of took different paths but stayed close friends. He save my hide a time or two and I hope I can repay the favor this time,"

Belinda gave him one of those I understand looks and went to get the coffee. She stopped about half way up the counter towards the kitchen.

"Is your friends name Bill?" she asked.

"How did you know?" Mike asked? She returned back and went up to Mike.

"Hi" she said as she held out her hand.

"You must be Mike."

Mike tilted his head in curiosity. "Yes I am, but how did you know my name?"

"Bill has been coming in almost every day for the same breakfast for quite some time now except I haven't seen him in a few days and I was worried something might have happened to him."

"Bill is in the hospital. Right now it looks like someone deliberately tried to run him over and for the moment he's in bad shape and in a medically induced coma."

"I knew something was wrong when he didn't show up funny but that might explain some things." said Belinda.

"What things and what do you mean by funny?" Mike asked.

"I don't mean laughing funny but strange funny." Belinda said.

"What do you mean strange funny? " Mike asked?

"Well" said Belinda. "Last week Bill and I were talking about you and he gave me a package to give to you in case anything ever happened to him." I asked him what did he mean and what was in the package and he just said you would know what to do with it. I asked him how would I ever get in touch with you and he said he was going to give me your address but he never got it to me and stopped coming in"

"Well where is it? " Mike asked.

"When Bill didn't show up the next day I went to the bank where I have my account and put it in my safe deposit box."

"Good move, I'll wait till you get off and go with you to go pick it up, if that's all right."

"I would like that, "Belinda said "In fact in lieu of what has happened I would like that a lot."

The next few hours seemed to drag on but soon it was four o'clock when Belinda got off work and met Mike. Mike accompanied Belinda to the bank. They pulled up to the bank and Mike noticed a dark black Chevy van sitting in the corner and he made a mental note of the van because he recalled seeing the same van outside Bills apartment earlier.

They went into the bank and one of the girls at one of the desks in the lobby asked if she could help.

"I would like to get into my safe deposit box." Belinda said.

The girl escorted Mike and Belinda to the vault, asked Belinda for her key and with the matching key opened the safe deposit box door, and let Belinda get the box out of the vault. Mike and Belinda went into one of those small rooms that all banks seem to have. Once inside Belinda opened the box and handed Mike a manila envelope. The envelope appeared to have been opened then resealed.

Mike opened the envelope and found a key for a storage box, a zippo lighter and an envelope marked Mike. Mike opened the envelope and took out the note that read:

"Mike if you are reading this I'm probably history. Don't forget the special times we had working on those cases way back when." The note was signed" your friend Baby Bill Halliday."

"Seems like your buddy had a premonition that something was about to happen." Belinda said.

"I didn't know his last name was Halliday or he was known as Baby Bill"

"Got any idea what the key might go to?'

"That is just Bills way of joking, even in a tough situation." said Mike.

"Baby Bill was what I called him. Don't have a clue to the key, but it must be something important."

Joe and Wayne arrived as Mike and Belinda were leaving the bank and asked Mike if he had found out anything?

"Seems like Bill had an inclining that something was about to happen and left me a note to that effect, along with a key to a lock box or something."

"How did you guys know we would be here anyway? Bill asked.

"We were heading to the station when we saw you come out of the bank." said Wayne.

Mike then showed Joe and Wayne the note.

"It seems like your buddy is the type of guy who has a sense of humor." Wayne said. "Maybe that's what this is all about, maybe he just ran into somebody who didn't have the same sense of humor."

"Let me give you a little advice Mike stay out of this. Just let us do our job or we will have to charge you with obstruction." Wayne said.

"Go sit with your buddy, he may not make it. Give us that key and we'll find out where that storage place it goes to and we will pick you up in the morning and we will see what's in it."

Mike gave Wayne the key and Joe and Wayne left.

He turned to Belinda.

"How about we pick up some groceries and I will make you my famous seafood surprise dish."

"OK there's a grocery store just down the street from Bills, we can probably get what you need there."

They stopped at the grocery store and Mike picked up a

jar of crushed garlic, some olive oil, and a jar of pasta sauce, some peppers, onions, a squash, a zucchini, some cherry tomatoes, some imitation seafood, and some angel hair pasta.

Back at Bills apartment while Belinda did some straightening up Mike went to work in the kitchen.

Mike chopped up the squash, zucchini, onions, peppers, and tomatoes, and sautéed them in olive oil and garlic while the angel hair pasta was cooking. He then added the imitation seafood and stirred in the pasta sauce along with some pepper, a pinch of salt and let it simmer a short time on low heat. After a short time, he spooned it out over the angel hair pasta and motioned to Belinda to come and sit down.

They tipped a glass of wine with a toast to Bill.

"This is Bills favorite dish," said Mike.

"I used to make this when we worked cases together. He never could cook anything"

They sat and shared some things about Bill and enjoyed the meal.

Later that night Belinda says "I really need to be at work early Mike. I enjoyed the evening. Maybe we could do this again when this is over."

"You got a date." said Mike.

After Belinda left, Mike sat around thinking about that note. "Baby Bill Halliday, what the heck was he trying to tell me" Mike thought to himself. He sat there thinking about it for a while and he remembered a drug case he and Bill had worked called the Baby Halliday case so called because the perpetrator had a baby face and no one suspected him of being a drug dealer.

"Why would Bill make a reference to that particular

case/? Mike wondered. Mike went over the case in his head. It wasn't a super special case. In fact, it was sort of a routine. It involved a low-level drug dealer who probably wouldn't have been caught had he not gotten so brazen. Seems the dealer had picked up a couple of bales of pot out in the everglades and was bringing it back to his apartment. Mike and Bill had been following him and would not have been able to stop him had he not forgotten to cover the pot. He had it in his pickup truck in the back in plain view like it was an ordinary bale of hay or feed when they pulled him over. They arrested him and got a warrant to search his apartment. He remembered that the dealer had hidden his books and cocaine way up in the air condition intake unit. In fact they had almost given up on finding anything when just by a freak accident one of them had kicked the big intake door in the wall next to the fire place the door fell open and out fell the evidence they were looking for..

He searched Bills apartment and found the intake unit in the hall. He got a chair opened the door, took out the filter and looked inside. There was nothing in site. I thought sure I would find something here, he thought to himself. He found a flash light and peered down the shaft. He noticed a thin piece of wire that ran down the shaft and disappeared around the corner. He gently pulled on the wire and after a short time he could see what appeared to be a small book. He pulled on the wire and got the book out to the end of the shaft and pulled it out. After retrieving the book he climbed down and opened it. Inside the book were several columns of writing. The first column was a date column including a day, month, and year. The second column had a first name and a last name. The third had a dollar amount that seemed to be in the millions, the fourth column listed a state and had short notations like LTO, MEG, or PB. Mike put the book back up in the vent, closed the filter door, put the chair back and laid back down on the couch. He felt the book would be safe with him here and the fact that the apartment had already been tossed and they didn't find the book meant that whoever was looking for the book probably figured that it wasn't there. He called the hospital to check on Bill and was told there was no change.

Eight o'clock the next morning the phone rang and it was Joe.

"Hey Mike, Wayne said he believes he knows where that locker is. We'll pick you up in about an hour at the dinner."

Mike showered, shaved, and hoofed it over to the dinner where Belinda was already hard at work.

"Sleep well? She asked.

"Like a baby." He answered.

"So now that you have had time to think about and have had some rest, do you have any idea what this is all about? She asked.

"Not a clue yet." said Mike.

"Have you figured out what he meant by special cases or why he left a lighter in there?"

"Nope, nothing has jumped into my mind as yet," said Mike.

"I need to call the hospital and check on Bill."

He called the hospital and talked to the doctor to make sure nothing had changed during the night and was told there was no change.

"He's important, doc so take good care of him."

Joe and Wayne came in sat down and Wayne asked." Found out anything new of interest Mike?"

"Like what?" said Mike?

"Hell I don't know maybe a journal or something that would give us a clue as to why all this is happening." Said Wayne.

"Wish I did but I didn't find a thing." says Mike. "Maybe we will find something in the storage unit. How did you figure out where it was anyway Wayne? Mike asked.

"Showed the key to a snitch of mine and he recognized the funny sign on the front of the key." Said Wayne.

Mike got into the back seat of the unmarked car with Joe and Wayne and headed to the storage unit.

"Mike have you got any ideas yet as to what this is all about?" asked Joe.

"Not yet, but I'm hoping something will change soon." Replied Mike as he leaned back in the seat.

"Funny I though you and Bill were close and yet you say Bill didn't leave you anything to let you know what this is all about." said Wayne.

"What are you trying to imply?" asked Mike. "Are you saying you think I'm holding out on you?"

"No not really, but I would of thought because you two were so close Bill would have said something." Said Wayne.

"He was about to tell me when that car struck him." said Mike.

The rest of the ride was silent until they reached the storage unit.

Mike got out while Joe and Wayne went into the office and got the manager. He told them where the unit was located.

They walked around to the back to unit 269. As they approached the locker, they notice that the lock had been cut off and was lying on the ground. They drew their weapons and Joe motioned to Wayne to lift the door as he covered him. Wayne bent down and slowly lifted the door.

"Looks like someone beat us to it." Said Joe.

"I'm not surprised." Said Mike.

"Someone has been one step ahead of us for a while." The room was one of those small units of ten feet by twelve feet with several eight foot tables some on top of each other. There appeared to be thirty or forty document like boxes that were filled with envelopes newspaper articles and memorabilia.

They looked at the boxes and stuff scattered all around on the floor. It looked like whoever had ransacked the place had a specific item they were looking for and just dumped box after box on the floor waded through the stuff and moved on to another box.

"Doesn't look like they found what they were looking for." said Joe.

"Maybe forensics can lift some prints."

"I also saw a security system in the office. Maybe we could catch a break," said Mike.

"I doubt it," said Wayne.

"Let's go see if the manager will let us have the tapes without a court order."

They go back to the office to question the manager.

"Have you seen anything unusual around here the last few days?" asks Joe.

"Well we had someone call in a bomb threat, but it turned out to be nothing," said the manager.

"The police department came and checked it out but found nothing." How about your security tapes? Can we take a look at them?" You can take the tapes but see that I get them back."

"Mind if I tag along and look at those tapes?" asked Mike.

"Wish we could Mike." said Joe.

"The captain would blow a gasket if he knew we let you see or tamper with the evidence. We'll drop you off at your place."

After they dropped him off Mike decided to go back to the storage unit and talk to the manager some more.

"Hey I was wondering if you might have remembered anything after we left that would help us out. Mike asked.

"No not really." says the manager.

"Is there anything on those tapes that may be able to help you out? He asked Mike.

"I didn't get a chance to see them yet," Says Mike.

"Well I have a back-up set here if you want to look at them."

"Back up set?" asked Mike.

"Yeh, I always back up my tapes on up and keep them for about a year or so in case I have any claims after the persons leave." said the manager.

"Thanks that would really help a lot." said Mike.

He spent the next few hours looking at the DVD's. When he got to the one that showed one lone person with a mask that entered the area and the first thing he did was spray paint the cameras so that not much more could be seen, but something on the DVD caught Mike/s eye. He ran the disc back and forth a few times and made note of what he saw. He couldn't quite make it out but it appeared to be some kind of chain with a pendant.

"Thanks he said to the manager. You've been a great help."

He headed back to the hospital to check on Bill, but stopped and made a call to an old friend in Miami first,

"Rick, can you lend me a hand for a few days? He asked the person on the other end.

"Be there tomorrow partner." was the reply.

After a brief visit with Bill at the hospital, Mike headed back to Bills place.

Mike called Belinda and she came over and brought a bottle of wine and some Chinese food. They sipped the wine, enjoyed the food and shared a good conversation. Belinda seemed real interested in the cases he and Bill had shared and Mike relayed some of the times they had enjoyed together. They spent several hours just sitting there with Mike telling her he didn't understand what Bill could have possibly gotten into to warrant his being killed.

"We had many cases together, but none that I could think of that would cause someone to kill either one of us."

"I can see why you are so upset about Bill being almost run over, but can we be making more of this than there really is Mike ?" she asked.

"Bill is the kind of a guy that always has a smile and something nice to say about everybody he meets. He's also a guy that takes care of things himself. For him to ask for my help lets me know this is serious. Whatever it takes to get to the bottom of this I'm in. No matter what I could always count on Bill and he can count on me to solve this. I'm not sure that we aren't taking this as serious as it is." Mike said,

"But I can assure you this; I won't stop till I get to the bottom of this, no matter what it takes."

The rest of the evening was spent making small talk. Belinda understood that when Mike got riled up he was no one to mess with and he seemed riled up now so she switched the conversation and just enjoyed each other's company. She poured them another small glass of wine and then reached over and shut off one of the lamps on the side of the couch. She got up and put on some soft music and said

"Not much more we can do tonight Mike," as she sat down beside him.

Later that evening when he was headed back to Bills place he thought to himself something just doesn't feel right. Things seemed to be going great yet there was that old gut feeling that Mike was experiencing that had never failed him before. He shrugged it off to the tension of the situation and after arriving at Bills place, took a shower and settled back for a good nights' sleep.

Chapter 5

The next day Mike met Rick at the airport. Coming through the airport concourse anybody looking at Rick could tell he was not the kind of guy who would shy away from a situation, but the kind of a guy you would want on your side in any emergency. Mike had met Rick when they were in combat together. Rick had grown up in the streets of Brooklyn and Queens and worked for the sanitation department before joining the Army. Rick was a former airborne member that Mike knew he could count on. Mike told Rick what he wanted and dropped him off at the hospital. Rick went up to the floor where Bill was located and arranged to secure the room next door. He checked all the exits and possible escape routes that one could use and then took up a position across the hall from Bills room. Mike in the meantime had taken a ride downtown to the Florida lottery, claims processing bureau on Marriot Drive.

He went inside and asked to speak to the person in charge. In just a short few minutes he was joined by a woman who projected control and knowledge. She was a middle age woman who had obviously taken care of herself. One who definitely presented herself as one who is in charge of the department. When she came over Mike presented his credentials and asked for a list of the past winners of the Lotto, Power Ball, and Mega money.

"Well we have a partial list of the winners, but remember the law allows the winners to remain anonymous. In fact we have only about five percent of the winning names."

"Well I'll take what you can give me. "Mike says.

She asked him to wait a few minutes so Mike took a seat and waited. It was only a matter of minutes before she reappeared and approached Mike. She handed Mike a small piece of paper with a list of names, addresses, and the weeks they won.

Mike took the list and looked them over. There were several people on the list that lived within a hundred miles of where he was so he decided to try to reach several of them. One of the names on the list was an address in nearby Dothan Alabama which was about a hundred miles away.

Mike decided he would stand out too much in the Corvette, so he rented a car and headed West on I-10 to Route 331 North. A short time later, he crossed over the state line and was in Dothan Alabama. Mike took out the list. The first name on the list was a Willie Tompkid at 520 Metropolitan Ct, Dothan Alabama. Mike punched the address into the GPS and pushed go. Heading up Route 231 in Alabama, Mike couldn't help but wonder what the names of the winners of the lotteries' of the States had to do with the attempts on his buddy. As he drove along, he thought Bill was never the kind of guy to gamble so I doubt it could have anything to do with his borrowing money. I know if he needed any money I'm sure he would have come to me. He would have told me if anyone was trying to shake him down and I can't see him doing anything that would warrant anybody being able to shake him down. No something is off kilter here and I aim to find the answer.

Well he thought maybe he could get some answers from this Willie Tompkid. As Mike cruised up the highway, he thought he noticed that a small SUV might be following him. He was just about to make a move to throw the follower off when the SUV turned left and no longer appeared in his rear view mirror. He kept glancing back to make sure the SUV hadn't pulled out and was behind him again. There were a few cars ahead of him but no one was behind him so he relaxed and put the rental car on cruise control and turned up the tunes on the satellite radio system.

After a short drive up Route 231 Mike turned off the road on to Forrest drive and then turned up on to Metropolitan Ct. Mike checked the house numbers 502,505, and 506 and that was it. It was a dead end street and there was no 520. Mike backed up to the house marked 506. He got out of the car, climbed the stairs and knocked on the door. The house was one of those two story southern homes that were built in the late fifties but were built solid with a southern charm. The porch surrounding the house was well maintained and Mike could see that the neighborhood was a quite one. He wondered why a lottery winner of a million dollars or more would stay here but reconciled himself to the fact it was probably home. He walked up onto the porch and knocked on the door. An elderly man appeared at the door and Mike said

"Sorry to bother you old timer but I'm looking for a Willie Tompkid who is supposed to live at 520 Metropolitan Ct."

"Never heard of him and there isn't any 520 unless it's that log out yonder." the gentleman replied.

"Have you lived here long?"

"Been here thirty five years and have never heard of anyone named Willie Tompkid or even anyone with a name that's even close to that. Why are you looking for this fellow anyway?"

Mike introduced himself showed the gentleman his credentials and told him he had gotten Willies name as a winner of the lottery some time back.

"Lottery winner? Around here? I don't think anyone around here has won. Shoot most folks around here are living on social security and barely are able to make ends meet. I'm sure if someone had won we would have known about it right away." said the gentleman.

Mike said

"Sorry to have bothered you partner I guess I have been given the wrong information."

He got back in the car and headed East on Route eighty four to the next town and name on the list he had gotten. It was listed as Joan Haddy, at two zero eight North East twentieth street Cairo Georgia. Cairo Georgia was a small town of approximately nine thousand people located about sixty miles west of Valdosta Georgia and about fifty miles north of Tallahassee Florida. North east twentieth street was located just about a half a mile from the center of the town. Mike looked it up on goggle on his phone and noted Cairo was known for just two things it seems. They had a Christmas parade that featured over seventy five floats every year in December and also had a antique automobile museum located there. As Mike drove the eighty miles or so on highway eighty four towards Cairo, he had an uneasy feeling that he was being followed again but didn't see any signs of a vehicle. He pulled off the highway at one point and waited a few minutes but no cars came by so he headed on to Cairo. By the time he got to Cairo he was getting hungry and stopped at a little home diner called the Smiling Skillet right on the highway on eighty four in Cairo. It was one of those diners you find when you travel that isn't a big chain name but almost always had good home cooking. The kind you could smell as you pulled into the parking area. It looked like a clean little place and a Mom and Pop dinner so he parked the rental and he went inside. There were several other cars in the parking lot that proved the down home cooking theory. A petite waitress who appeared to be about fortyish with long hair that was covered up with a hair net came over pulled a pencil from her ear, held out her order pad and said.

"Would you like some coffee?" She had a nametag on the read Sam.

"Please." he said.

"I would also like some information if I can. Have you lived here long and do you know most of the people here? "Mike asked.

"Well I was born here but just came in off the road. Because we are a small community most of the families here we all know each other," She said.

"Came off the road? Oh drove one of those big rigs over the road?"

"For over twenty years." "Don't think I could handle that, too many bad drivers who don't seem to care about anything but getting there yesterday."

"It can be a challenge but it paid the bills for several years."

Mike ordered an egg white western omelet and started to talk to Sam and found out that was short for Samantha. He found out she was actually in her early sixties and had to give up driving to raise her two grand children and take care of her husband who had recently came down with a heart problem. Mike paused to reflect on how lucky his own life had been and how things might have been different under some other circumstances. He called Sam over and asked her if she knew a Joan Haddy.

"Never heard of her," Sam replied.

"Where would I find the two hundred block of North East Twentieth Street? Mike asked.

"Smack in the middle of Greenwood Cemetery." She said.

"In the middle of the cemetery, you sure?" he asked.

"See for yourself, your about a half mile away heading east on eighty four on your left side." Mike finished his breakfast got a coffee to go and headed out the door.

Mike headed the rental east on eighty four and turned left on north east twentieth street and sure enough was right at the entrance to Greenwood Cemetery.

Chapter 6

Around what would have been the two hundred block he found a headstone with the name Joan Haddy on it, who had passed away ten years prior to winning the lottery according to the date on the headstone. This is getting stranger by the minute he thought. He headed back to the diner to talk to Sam. All the way back he still had that uneasy feeling that someone was keeping an eye on him, but he didn't notice any vehicles following him. Back at the diner once again he called Sam over.

"Sam is there anyone around the area who might have known Joan Haddy" he asked. "Well" she replied,

"There is an old timer who comes around here every day around this time and talks about how he's been here his whole life and wishes it would have stayed the way it used to be. He should be in now any minute. He always orders a glass of water and eats the crackers on the table. We've kind of have grown used to him and let him sit here".

Mike ordered another cup of coffee sat back and waited. About fifteen minutes later an old man with a cane came into the diner and sat down in the first booth. He appeared to be frail and under nourished but walked with his head held high and a firm step. He was wearing a ball cap hat with a military insignia indicating he was former military, worn out jeans and a suit jacket that had seen better days. Mike noticed that his toes were beginning to stick out of his shoes. He was a scruffy looking gentleman about five foot five and a little on the frail side. One could tell that under that hat was a person who had experienced many trials and tribulations. The waitress came over and had his water. Mike eased over to the booth and asked the old timer if it was ok if he joined him. The old timer nodded and Mike sat down and held out his hand.

"Mike Franklin," he said and introduced himself. The old man extended his hand "Tommy Rich" he said,

"And I'm not rich by any means."

Mike told Tommy that he was a private eye from Miami and was there on a case.

"Tommy can I buy you lunch and ask you a few questions? Throw in coffee and I'll answer any thing you can ask."

Sam came over and Mike said

"Give him what he wants and put this on my tab."

The old guys eyes lit up like he had just won the lotto and ordered a chicken dinner with potatoes, salad, string beans and even a bowl of soup. After Sam brought the soup and Tommy had eaten about half a bowl he turned to Mike and said

"What do you want to know?" "Did you ever hear of anyone named Joan Haddy?" "Sure" he replied

"In fact I dated her once a long time ago, but she passed away."

When did she die?"

"About ten years ago. Her granddaughter came to visit and she had a heart attack and passed. Strange to because she never mentioned that she had a grand-daughter and no one knew she had a heart problem."

"Do you recall what her grand-daughters name was?'

"Seems like it was, Linda, or Brenda or something like that."

Mike showed Tommy a picture he had taken on his cell phone of Belinda.

"Look anything like her?"

"She resembles her but this girl is much older and her hair isn't the same. Could be but I'm not sure.

"Thanks Tommy you've been a great help."

Before leaving the diner, he gave Sam two hundred and fifty bucks.

"See that he get a few lunches when he comes in and call me when that runs out."

He gave Sam his cell number as well as his office number in Miami.

He had one more address to check out before heading back to Tallahassee. This one was nearby in Moultrie Georgia. The next name on the list was a Robert Boretska located at two thousand one hundred and two South Vanderberg Drive, Moultrie Georgia. He drove east again until he ran into highway three nineteen heading north. The State of Georgia was in the process of redoing the roads so what should have been a half hour ride took an hour and a half. He headed north about twenty-five miles to Moultrie on highway three nineteen until he reached state highway one thirty three. He turned south and ran about five miles until he ran into South Vanderberg Drive. Again, he had that hair on the back of your neck feeling that someone was following him but didn't see anyone. An hour later Mike pulled up to the address, he had for Robert Boretska. The address he had, turned out to be the State Prison located on south Vanderberg Drive. Mike got out of the rental and went inside to the desk showed his credentials and asked if they had an inmate named Robert Boretska.

"Sure." The officer at the desk said.

"He's been a prisoner for the last ten years and he'll be here compliments of the state for the next twenty years."

"Do you think I could I see him? " Mike asked.

"Have to ask the warden." He said.

Mike met the warden and after showing him his private investigator credentials and explaining, he was a former police officer and was working on a possible homicide case the warden agreed to let Mike talk to the inmate. Robert Boretska came into the interview room. He was a small frail man that looked to be in his early fifties. He sat down across from Mike and picked up the phone on the other side of the thick glass that separated the guests from the prisoners. Mike picked up the accompanying phone.

"Robert I'm Mike Franklin from Miami and I'm a private detective working on a possible homicide case and your name surfaced during my investigation.

"I don't know anything about any homicide."

"Good but answer a few questions and I'll add a hundred to your credit account here."

"Go ahead."

"Ever live in Tallahassee?" Mike asked.

"Yeh, I did but that was fifteen years ago. I worked for the state of Florida. I worked in the capitol building, as a maintenance guy."

"Ever play the lotto?" asked Mike.

"Sure almost every week, but didn't do any good though, although I did win five hundred bucks one time. I had to go upstairs and collect it. Hell they wanted to know all about me. If I had a family, if I grew up in the area. Hell you would have thought I was applying for the secret service or something."

"Well did you grow up in Tallahassee? What about your family?

"Don't have any, grew up in a small town in Connecticut, and never knew any family. The boy's home I grew up in said I was found on the steps of a church. They took me in and I grew up in an orphanage and took the last name of one of the counselors there."

"How did you end up in here?" Mike asked.

"Well no one would believe me but I was set up. One day after I had finished my shift, I went into the locker room and took a shower as I always did before going home. I always shower at work because I have such low water pressure at home. This shower at work always had plenty of flow and hot water. After I finished my shower, I went to my locker and noticed someone had put a package way in the back. I almost didn't see it. Looking back now I guess while I was working someone put it in my locker. I reached in, picked it up and started to look at it when all of a sudden two guys grabbed me threw me against the locker and said I was under arrest for distributing cocaine. I tried to tell them I didn't know anything about any cocaine or the package but they said they were tipped off by an informant who bought some coke off me. I didn't have any money for a good lawyer and the public defender they gave me was a new one who had just passed the bar exam. In fact I was his first case. The judge was up for reelection and he made an example of me."

"Did they ever say how they came to look in your locker? Asked Mike.

"They said they were acting on a anonymous tip." "Did your lawyer get the informant up on the stand and question him about the deal?" asked Mike.

"He overdosed before my lawyer could talk to him but they had a written statement they used at the trial."

"Maybe when I get through with this I can help." Mike said.

"Well I ain't going anywhere."

Mike got in the rental and headed back to Tallahassee.

A few hours later he arrived at the hospital and went up to the room and checked in with Rick.

"Is everything all right Rick?" Mike asked?

Rick gave Mike that I'm not sure look and Mike said.

"What is it Rick?"

"Nothing concrete but those two detectives seemed to have a real interest in him. In fact, the one named Wayne was in here and seemed startled when I came out of the bathroom. He said he was just concerned about Bill but I had an uneasy feeling about him."

"Yeh I'm beginning to get that same feeling. Keep your eyes open."

As he left the room, Mike made a mental note to have a talk with Wayne later on.

He called up Belinda and asked her if she was free for dinner.

"Always, for you Mike." She said.

"There's a little Italian restaurant a couple of miles from here and they are known to have the best food in town. It's called Francescos.

"I'm familiar with the restaurant. They have one in Ocala where a friend of mine lives. I've heard they are very good but have never eaten there."

Mike picked her up and they went to a small Italian restaurant. It was in one of those small strip malls. They went in and were seated in a few minutes. It appeared small from the outside but once inside Mike could see there was a bar area as well as a dining area with cozy booths. It was an open floor plan where the kitchen was in full view of the customers. In a short time, they were seated and ordered a glass of wine while looking over the menu and deciding what they were going to try. Mike had the chicken and linguini with sweet red peppers in a crème sauce and Belinda had the angel hair pasta and a red clam sauce. While they were eating, Belinda asked how it was going and Mike told her he was making progress and was going to talk to Wayne about some things that were bothering him the next day.

"What things? She asked?

"Nothing I can prove at this time, just some things that don't seem to add up, along with some hunches." He said.

After dinner Mike drove her to her apartment.

"Care to come up for a night cap? She asked.

"I can't think of any reason not to." he said. As they entered the apartment Mike couldn't help but notice that this was an oversize apartment decorated very richly and he couldn't help but wonder how she could afford such furnishings on a waitress salary. He decided that maybe she had received an inheritance or maybe she was sharing it with a friend. Either way he decided that now was not the time to question how or when. Belinda poured them both a glass of wine put on some music and excused herself for a minute. When she returned she had slipped into something more shall we say comfortable. She sat down beside him and said, "Let's make a memory.

Later on in Bills apartment, he kicked back and thought, "I could get used to this."

It was about six o'clock when Mike got up. He put on some coffee and jumped in the shower. After a quick breakfast he headed over to Wayne's house on Perkins Avenue. As he was coming down Wayne's street, he noticed a black SUV pulling away. He made a mental note to ask Wayne about the SUV because it was similar to the one he thought was following him a few times. As he was pulling up to Wayne's house he noticed Wayne was on the front porch, he seemed to be staggering. He pulled up to the house and he heard Wayne call out something and at the same time he heard the blast that leveled Wayne's house and threw Wayne about fifteen feet down the lawn. The explosion knocked Mike off his feet and onto the ground. Several pieces from the explosion hit Mike's car but didn't hit him, but the explosion left a ringing in his ears. Immediately the house was engulfed in flames that shot out at least thirty feet high.

Mike jumped from his car and ran over to Wayne and dragged him away from the burning house. Wayne was badly hurt and Mike could tell he didn't have much time. He cradled Wayne in his arms and asked him,

"Who did this to you Wayne"?

Wayne coughed and said in a barely audible voice.

"Mike be careful, they want you out of the way."

"I got in too deep, and couldn't get out."

"Who are they? Mike asked.

"I took orders from my boss, but that's just the tip of the iceberg. It goes way up there Mike."

Wayne's body went limp and he was starting to lose consciousness so mike shook him a little. His eyes opened up once again.

"Is Joe a part of this?" Mike asked.

Wayne mouthed,

"No he didn't have a clue" then slumped down as he passed away in Mikes arms. By this time, Mike was hearing sirens coming from what seemed like all directions. Within minutes Mike was surrounded by the paramedics and fire fighters who seemed to arrive simultaneously. Before the trucks had even came to a stop the firefighters were pulling the hoses off the back of the trucks and heading towards the burning building. A second later, they were dousing the flames with water from the trucks. At the same time, the paramedics had pulled up and came rushing over to Mike with a defibrillator in hand, had ripped open Wayne's shirt and were trying to shock him back to life. They tried for a few minutes but were unsuccessful. They turned towards Mike and shook their head.

A few minutes later Joe arrived on the scene and said "What happened?"

"I'm afraid Wayne was into something heavy Joe and it caught up with him."

"Hey I don't like what you are implying Mike. I worked with him and at times he seemed a little worried about something, but I attributed it to the job. If you know something else I sure would like to hear about it."

"Well when I pulled up he was still conscience but barely able to speak and as I held him and tried to comfort him he whispered to me to be careful that they want me dead. He also said he got in too deep."

"What was he into Mike? Joe asked. And who is they?"

"I'm not completely sure just yet, but I'm going to find out." Mike answered.

"Does this have anything to do with Bills accident? " Joe asked.

"Yes it's all tied in together, but I'm not sure just how the pieces fit yet."

"How can I help?" Joe asked.

"What can you tell me about Wayne" asked Mike.

"Well we've been partners for about nine years. Ever since I made detective, but Wayne is a loner and while he accepted us working together he always seemed to resent working with a partner."

"He kept mostly to himself on his time off,"

"Did he have any money problems? Did he take vacations or time off?"

He seemed to have plenty of money when he needed it, and one time he got a little upset with me when I asked how he could afford some of the things he had like a new car every year, and how he could afford to take those long weekends and go down to Florida every few weeks. He told me to mind my own business and that he budgeted for those things. After that I didn't bring it up."

"Did he handle any high profile cases?" Mike asked.

"We drew our fair share of cases but nothing spectacular. In fact the biggest case he had is the one that got him that detective badge, but that was before he and I were partners."

"What case was that?" Mike asked.

"Don't know that much about it, he didn't talk about it but I heard he busted a big cocaine dealer that worked at the Capital as a maintenance guy that was a big distributer.

I understand they caught the guy with two kilos of cocaine in his locker. When they searched the guy's house they found ten more kilos. The guy swore he didn't know any- thing about cocaine, but you know how they lie."

"The attorney general was so impressed he personally promoted Wayne to detective first grade."

"Who was the Attorney General"? Mike asked.

"Pete McArthur" Joe said.

"Is he still around?" Mike asked.

"Well he retired from the Attorney Generals office and took a cushy position as head of the lottery division. I guess part of his responsibility is handing out the dough to the winners."

"What do you know about this Pete McArthur?" Mike asked.

"Tell you the truth, not much. I think he was a hot shot attorney in Miami."

"Miami? Are you sure?" asked Mike.

"I'm positive Mike. I heard some of the other guys at the station talking about him and they said they didn't know much but at one time he was under suspicion for something or other."

"Did anybody know what he was suspected of?" asked Mike.

"There was a lot of speculation but no one seemed to have any details about anything just hearsay, but you know how that is."

"Yes I do listen I'll catch up with you later. Keep me up to date on Wayne's murder investigation."

"Murder, are you sure? What makes you think it was murder? I thought it was an accident." Joe asked.

"I don't have any concrete proof right now, but my gut tells me something isn't right. I know it may seem strange, but do me a favor and approach it that way. See what you can find out about Wayne. In the meantime I'll check my sources in Miami concerning Pete." Mike said.

"OK. I'll do that," Joe said."

"I'll catch up with you later."

Mike went back to the hotel and made a phone call to his old friend Judge Ed David. Judge David's secretary answered the phone and Mike asked her if he could talk to the judge. She said,

"Just a minute." and put him on hold.

Mike had met Judge David back when he was an upcoming lawyer with the States Attorneys office. Mike knew him to be a fair and honest attorney then and a good judge now. One who was firm in his convictions but also one who was fair under the law. One who believed in giving a person every opportunity to do right but stern on one who broke the law deliberately. A short minute later, Judge David came on the phone, and said, "Mike been a while. What's the occasion? Remember you still owe me a dinner."

"I may owe you a month of dinners after this one Ed. I'm up in Tallahassee and Bills in a coma and it just gets worst from there."

"How can I help Mike?"

"What do you know about a Pete McArthur?" Mike asked.

"Rumored to be the next Attorney General of the United States at one time, but had a little trouble a few years back."

"What kind of trouble?" Mike asked.

"Again Mike just a rumor, but word was that while he was in the public Defender's office he got in pretty deep with the Cuban Mafia and ended up being their biggest asset. Rumer had it that he was fixing cases involving cocaine dealers although there was never any proof or any charges brought up. Seems like several dealers got off on technicalities when they came up before him as a judge. Word was he was into them for several million from his use of cocaine and might be indicted when all of a sudden he got that job in Tallahassee as the head of the lottery division. At one time he was linked to a murder investigation of an escort but that seemed to not pan out because the escort didn't seem to have any relatives and no one claimed the body and the few witnesses all disappeared before he could be charged.. Any way since he left here not much has been heard from him. So what does he have to do with Bill?"

"I'm not completely sure, but this does clear up the picture some-what." Mike said.

"Well let me know if you need some help. The head of the Federal Bureau of Investigation is an old card playing buddy of mine."

"Thanks judge that might just be something I need." Mike said and hung up.

He decided to get some sleep and start fresh in the morning.

Chapter 7

Mike heard a knock on the door and looked at the clock on the side of his bed. It showed the time was eight thirty. Mike had slept all night without ever waking up once. He peered through the peephole and saw Joe on the other side. He opened the door and Joe walked in with a tray of coffee and donuts. "I figured you could use a cup of coffee. " Joe said. "You're here bright and early." Mike said.

"Yes, I had a hard time sleeping." Joe said.

"That doesn't sound like you, how come?" Mike asked.

"Well I pulled a couple of strings and looked into Wayne's bank accounts." Joe said.

'Well did you find anything interesting?" Mike asked.

"Either he had a rich uncle I didn't know about or he hit the lotto and didn't tell anybody." Joe said. "He has over five hundred thousand dollars in a couple of different accounts. Mike I don't have any idea where he got that kind of cash. He was always saying he was barely making it Mike but he was socking away at least five grand a week from somewhere."

Just about that time there was another knock on the door.

Mike looked at Joe, and they both reached for their guns and Mike slowly made his way over to the door and looked out the peephole. On the other side he saw two guys in suites and one of them was holding up an identification packet that showed he was with the federal bureau of investigation.

Mike opened the door and the one with the ID said.

"Hi. Mike Franklin"? He asked.

"That's me." Mike said.

"To what do I owe a visit from the Federal Bureau of Investigation.?" Mike asked.

"Can you come down to the Bureau with us Mike our director would like to talk to you?" "I need to check on my friend Bill first and then I will be happy to go with you." Mike said.

"If you don't mind we will tag along just to see that you don't get lost." The agents said.

Mike put in a call to Rick at the hospital.

"How is he doing Rick? Mike asked.

"He's still in a coma Mike."

"How about you Rick are you OK?" Mike asked.

"Yeah, I'm fine. " Rick replied.

"I had a couple of my boy's come up to help and set up a round the clock on him. Have you learned anything yet?' Rick asked.

"No not yet Rick, but I'm here with a couple of Federal Bureau of Investigation guys that want to talk to me so I'll let you know something as soon as I can."

"Not to worry Mike all is well here." Rick said.

After hanging up from Mike Rick heads back to Bills room. As he approaches the room, one of his guys motions to the maintenance guy pushing the laundry cart past the nurse's station and approaching Bills room. Rick and his helper start towards the maintenance guy who suddenly pushes the cart at them and takes off running.

"Stay with Bill," Rick yells out and takes off running after the guy. As he rounds the corner, he is met with a "pop, pop" and two thuds in the wall over his shoulder. He immediately draws his gun from his belt and ducks down and returns fire.

The maintenance guy pushes the door open to the stairway and heads down the stairs with Rick in hot pursuit. Pop pop, the gunman fires. Blam, blam comes the sound from Ricks gun. The gunman exits on the ground floor with Rick in pursuit. He runs out the door and jumps into a waiting dark colored SUV and fires two more shots, pop, pop, as the SUV speeds off.

Rick returns to the room and checks on Bill who is OK and still in the medical induced coma. He puts in a call to Mike.

"Mike we just had an incident."

"What do you mean incident? What kind of incident?" Mike asks.

"Looks like someone has put out a contract on Bill but we caught up to it in time."

"Is Bill OK?" Mike asks.

"Yeah he's fine but we just might be able to use a little more help here." Rick says.

"What happened?" Mike asks.

Rick tells Mike what transpired and a few minutes later Mike says

"OK keep a good watch on him, I'm here at the Federal Bureau of Investigation building I'll get back at you as soon as I can."

Mike tells the two F.B.I. agents what happened.

The two agents lead Mike into the Directors office. Sitting behind the desk is a tall solid built man with a touch of grey in his hair that looked to be about fifty.

"Hi Mike I'm Francis Kaplin the director here in the Northeast district." Is your friend Bill Ok? "

"He's fine for now, but this is getting bigger by the minute and I might need reinforcements." Mike said as he tells the director of the latest incident that occurred at the hospital with Bill.

The director pushed a button on the bottom of his desk and two agents appeared.

"Go assist Mikes people at the hospital and check everybody coming in or out. I want that hospital locked up tight and Bill to have maximum protection until this is over." said the director.

"What the heck is going on?" Mike asked.

"Well Mike we've been watching Wayne for about six months now." said the director.

"Why?" asked Mike.

"Well we suspect is that he was getting paid off to keep quiet about an operation involving the director of the lottery, the Mexican drug cartel and possibly someone else."

"What kind of operation?" Mike asked.

"Can't really say right now, but your friend Bill contacted us a few months ago and said he had discovered some evidence that pointed to the Director. The attorney General was preparing a case against Pete McArthur when you came up to meet Bill."

"That explains some things." Mike said.

"What things, can you shed any light on the subject?" asked Francis.

"I'm getting close to being able to nail this shut for you. As soon as I'm sure of my hunch I'll bring you up to speed with all I know. Right now it's just speculation."

"OK Mike." The director says I checked out your background with an old attorney friend of mine Ed David and he vouched for you. Remember though this is an active F.B.I. investigation so keep me in the loop."

On the way back to Bills apartment Mike puts in a call to Joe and asks him to meet him there. As he pulls into the complex, he notices that things seem to be returning to normal. There are people coming and going. The cable guy is there and children are playing touch football and having fun. Seems the only problem is the TV cable is not working but the cable truck tell him they are working on it because as Mike pulls into the complex he notices several cable trucks and thinks they must have had a major problem with the television reception in the area. Mike enters the apartment and gets up into air condition vent area and retrieves the book he found earlier. He opens the book and turns a few pages and notices there are two totals in the amount column. One of the columns seems to be a total of the money column, and one that has a total with one hundred thousand dollars less. He turns the page and finds the same results. There are two columns of money entries on each page. One total in the money column, and then underneath the total is another column that is a one hundred thousand dollars subtraction and then a new total. Mike also notices that each total is split into two equal parts. One marked XEM and one marked AIC. He also notices that in the back of the book are two addresses. One located in Mexico, and one located in Ocala Florida. The one in Ocala is located at an air ranch just south of the city. Mike spends a few minutes looking at the book then takes out his phone and takes some pictures of the pages and sends them back to his secretary's e-mail hoping she can make some sense of what he has found. He then puts the book back up in the air vent, screws the vent back into place and then he gives Joe a call.

"Are you getting close buddy?" Mike asks.

"Very close in fact I'm coming into the complex as we speak." Joe replies.

Mike goes over to the door and opens it for Joe. As Joe approaches, Mike notices that the cable truck doesn't have anyone around it. Joe pulls up and they both go inside.

"Hey Joe have you noticed there seems to be a cable problem around here?"

"Yeah, I heard they are having trouble in this area." Joe says as he puts his finger to his lips to indicate to Mike to be quite.

Joe then pulls out an instrument out of his jacket that looks like a set of head phones attached to a curling iron. He quickly moves around the room indicating to Mike that the apartment seems to be bugged and points out a couple of microphones. They both head outside and as they approach the cable truck it takes off at a high rate of speed. They notice that it doesn't have a license plate on it.

They go back to the apartment and Joe makes a call and puts out an all points bulletin on the truck. Soon there is a team there that arrives and sweeps the apartment and finds four electronic listening devices.

"Mike what the heck is going on?" Joe asks.

"I don't have all the answers just yet Joe but let's go meet with the F.B.I. director and I'll fill you in on all I know." Mike says.

Mike and Joe met at the reception desk by the director and a woman. She is dressed in a professional manner and Mike could tell she was the type that one didn't want to get on the bad side of. She presented herself as a intelligent person who knew her business whatever that was.

Francis says to Mike

"I'd like you to meet Miss Katie Howard, the United States Attorney's office for district five which includes Tallahassee. She will be heading the investigation from the Attorney Generals side. There appears to be a connection between our investigation and an ongoing investigation regarding the Central Intelligence Agency and a few rogue agents. The central intelligence agency has lost contact with a few agents and they have been trying to reel them in to no avail. Seems these agents have somehow discovered a scheme to gather millions of dollars for themselves and have gone underground.

As they all sit down, they are joined by a stenographer. Mike begins to relay the information he found in the book left at Bills townhouse apartment. He tells how the book has addresses and names of former lotto winners and that only about one out of ten winners is an actual person and usually just for a small jackpot but how the big jackpots go to people who are never seen or heard of or who appear to be deceased. Mike explains that it appears the lotto director was skimming off the top before he made payoffs to two groups the XEM's and the AIC's.

"Mike I need that book," Katie says.

"Maybe it will end all this and Bill will be safe. In the meantime I'll get a warrant for McArthur and have him picked up."

She made a call and then she headed over to see the judge while Francis told a couple of agents to follow him. Then he, the agents, Joe and Mike headed over to the apartment complex where Bill lives.

As they approached the complex, they noticed several fire trucks at the complex. Pulling into the complex, they are met by the fire captain and they discover that there was an explosion in the complex and that fire had destroyed Bills apartment.

"What happened?" The F.B.I. director asked the fire chief.

"Can't say right now, but it looks like a gas line got loose and somehow ignited." said the fire chief. "It looks like that book is history now Mike." Says the director,

"That can't be a coincidence." says Mike.

"Any chance we can nose around in this?" they asked the fire chief.

"Not right now we have to be sure everything is safe and turned off." Says the fire chief.

"Well maybe we can break McArthur and get him to talk." said the director. They head back to the office where McArthur is waiting for them.

"Francis" Mike says "I would like to be in that room with you." Francis hesitates for a few seconds and then says "Maybe that will sway him a little."

They enter the interrogating room where Pete is sitting

across the table with a smug look on his face as if to say you have nothing on me that you can prove. While Mike stands off to the side Francis says to McArthur

"Pete I need to advise you of your rights, You have the right to," McArthur stops the director saying,

"Yes I know I have the right to remain silent, and I'm invoking that right as of now." "Pete we have you on enough to send you away for the rest of your life. You know how this goes, cooperate and maybe we can get you into the witness protection program. We've already searched your bank account records and have found several million dollars along with several aliases and bank accounts out of the country. So help yourself and maybe we can make some kind of a deal. The United States attorney is waiting outside to put it in writing."

"I want my attorney." says McArthur.

"He can't help you on this one Pete." Francis says.

"We'll see." says McArthur, "I want my attorney."

The director and Mike walk out of the room and the director says to an agent.

"Put him in a cell till his attorney gets here."

The agent takes him away and puts him in a cell.

"We sure could use that book Mike." Francis says.

Pete's attorney arrives and advises Pete not to answer any more questions.

Pete is brought back into a holding cell to await a hearing.

The next day Pete is arraigned and given a two million dollar bail and ordered to surrender his passport. As he leaves the courtroom, he smirks at Mike and Francis.

"Well Mike, we will see you at the trial, and in the

meantime if you come up with any more information give me a call. Here is my cell number." says Francis. Mike goes back to Bills apartment to see if he can gain any insight as to what happened. He goes into the apartment and although there is a lot of damage the air conditioner vent although charred from the fire appears to have escaped serious damage. He looks into the air condition vent and pulls out the book, which although damaged still has pages that are legible and might still be useful. He decides to give what is left of the book to Francis to see if the F.B.I. lab can pull anything out of the remains. Mike calls up Belinda and asks her if she would like to go to dinner.

"Just name the time and place and I'll meet you there." Belinda says.

"Where would you suggest?" Mike asks.

"There's a great restaurant at the Hotel Duval called Shula's 347 Grill Mike. I though you would like a taste of home. I'll meet you there at seven thirty." "That sounds great, I'll see you there." Mike says.

"Hi Mike, long time no see." Belinda said as she arrived at the restaurant. She had on one of those famous long black dresses that every woman wants to wear but some can't. "Wow what's the occasion? Mike asked.

"None, just wanted to make sure you don't forget me. I haven't seen much of you lately, what's been happening?

"Sorry I haven't gotten in touch lately, but things have been a little crazy. It seems the lottery director was on the take and associated with either organized crime or some other high power."

Well what is he saying"?

"Nothing yet his lawyer had bailed him out and he has him under wraps, but he knows how it works in a situation like this."

"How's that "? Belinda asked.

"Well in any criminal situation like this the first one who agrees to testify gets the deal and I think this Pete might just be willing to co-operate once he realizes that a life out west under the federal witness protection plan is better that a life time in prison. I'm sure his lawyer will convince him that a deal is in his best interest."

"Do you really think that there is a possibility he will give up his associates considering the seriousness of the consequences?"

"What do you mean by consequences?"

"I'm just guessing here but from what you said, I would bet that if he talks to the federal bureau of investigation and these people that are involved are well connected he probably won't last very long."

"I think if he has any chance to avoid a long prison term he will cooperate with the federal government. That way I'm sure with a good lawyer he might just be given a new identity and put in the witness protection plan where he just might be able to live out the rest of his years. One thing is for sure if he doesn't cooperate with them he is looking at a long, long prison term and like you say if this is so well connected he won't last a month before somebody kills him. I think he's between a rock and a hard place either way."

"That is if he has a good lawyer Mike because some of them are just rookies and don't know the ropes."

"Well this McArthurs lawyer is Percey Frinkel a lawyer

who used to be pretty sharp. I hear he worked somewhere in Georgia and was quite successful in the States Attorney's office until he retired to go fishing. I hear he was good at that also. Hey you seem to be really getting interested in this case?"

"Well I've never known a private detective before and the whole thing is kind of exciting Mike. I can see how you would enjoy the thrill of it all."

"I guess I have been doing it so long I don't think of it as thrilling but as sometimes bad things seem to happen to good people and everybody needs a little help once in a while."

"I'm sure it will all turn out for the better Mike. Or at least the way it should, please excuse me a minute Mike I have to go to the powder room."

"Sure can I order you a glass of wine"?

"Please and we can have a nice quite dinner afterwards"?

Mike orders a glass of white zinfandel for Belinda and a glass of bourbon and water for himself and after about ten minutes Belinda returns and says,

"Mike I apologize but I got into a conversation with an old friend of mine that I haven't seen in a long time and time slipped away."

"Not to worry." Mike says.

"Let's just sit and have a nice dinner and enjoy the evening."

"Sounds good Mike here's to a great meal and"?

"I'll drink to that."

The waiter comes over and Mike asks,

"What's good tonight"?

"Well sir we have a grilled salmon stuffed with crab that sells very well and seems to be a favorite."

"What do you think Belinda?

"That sure sounds good to me."

"Great make that two."

As the waiter leaves Mike raises his glass and sys" To a special night." Belinda raises her glass and says

"I hope so."

Almost an hour goes by and Mike and Belinda are just about through.

"What say we go up to your place and complete the night"? Mike says.

Belinda just smiles. Mike calls the waiter over and gives him his credit card to pay the bill. A minute later, the waiter returns and hands Mike the bill and a pen. Just as Mike signs the bill, his phone rings. He looks at the name and says to Belinda

"Sorry I've got to take this." Francis Kaplin the director says to Mike,

"Mike can you meet me at the McArthur house."

"Sure but can you tell me what's going on Francis"?

"Never mind, just meet me there as soon as you can."

Mike hangs up the phone and says to Belinda.

"I'm sorry but I'll have to take a rain check."

"What happened"?

"I don't know yet but that was the director of the federal bureau of investigation and it seems urgent I'll call later."

Mike jumps into the Corvette and heads over to McArthurs house. As he arrives, he sees Francis talking to a police officer and notices that there are multiple F.B.I. cars along with several police cars and several EMT's along with Joe the detective. Kaplin motions to Mike to come over and signals to the police officers to let Mike cross the familiar yellow tape the covers all crime scenes.

"What has happened Francis"? Mike asks?"

"Let's go inside and I'll show you."

They go inside and there in the living room is Pete McArthur with a gun in his right hand and half of his head blown off.

"Looks like he decided his life was over." Francis says.

"I don't think so." says Joe.

"He was left-handed, and couldn't do anything with his right hand. He couldn't even hold a spoon and in fact one time when he injured his left hand he had to hire someone to help feed him for a few days while his hand healed. He had some kind of nerve damage in his right hand from a childhood accident.

"Well now we have a real problem on our hands. He was our best chance of getting to the bottom of all this and finding out who was the head of this operation. It looks like we are back to square one. Hope the lab comes up with something." Francis says.

"Keep me in the loop will you Francis. I have to go to the hospital and pick up Bill they say he is well enough to go home for now. So I'm going to pick him up and head home."

"Mike we still have to search that air ranch in Ocala. Care to join us"?

"Sounds like a plan Francis, I'll pick up Bill and gather my stuff at the hotel and we'll meet you there in Ocala at the air ranch tomorrow."

"See you there in the morning mike." Francis says.

Mike decides to call Belinda to renew the date that was

abruptly interrupted. He dials Belinda's number, it rings three times then goes to the message mode. He explains that he has to head back to Miami but would like to see her before he leaves. He leaves his number and asks her to call.

Chapter 8

Mike heads back to the hospital where to his surprise Bill is sitting up and eating. "Good to see you buddy I thought I had lost you there for a few days."

"Mike what has happened?"

"A ton buddy." Mike sits down and proceeds to tell Bill all that has happened and asks him if he remembers about the book and what got him there.

"Mike I don't remember a thing except being hit by that car. I wish I could remember something that might help solve this mystery but I can't think of anything that might be pertinent to this mystery."

"Don't worry about it buddy, you just come back to Miami with me and stay until you feel up to something else and in the meantime you can help me."

Mike tells Bill about the air ranch in Ocala and that they are going to meet with Francis the next day and see if it will add anything that would lend to the closing of this or at least give them a clue as to who the higher ups are."

Mike puts in a call to Belinda but she doesn't answer so

he leaves her a message telling her he has to go back to Miami and is stopping at the Ocala air ranch and meeting the F.B.I. director there in the morning and tells her to call him back when she gets a chance. He promises her that he will return and make up for lost time when this is all over. He and Bill head back to the hotel to get a good night's sleep before they head south.

"Got any idea what this is all about Mike and why am I so important that there seems to be a premium on killing me?"

"Well old buddy near as I can figure it out somehow the names you found in that book belong to some group of people or organization that was skimming money from the weekly lotto and dividing it up among themselves."

"How the heck could they do that and who are they?"

Haven't figured that out yet partner but maybe tomorrow will shed some light on the why and wherefores. For now, let's just try to get a good night's sleep. Glad to see you back on this planet"

They get up early next morning and head east. They pull onto interstate ten and head east. They reach interstate seventy-five and head south. After about an hour, they stop at a Cracker Barrel restaurant and have some breakfast and mike again tries Belinda's phone. He gets the answering message and leaves her a message telling her he will call her later that night. Mike hands the phone off to Bill and says,

"I keep getting funny sounds from that thing and I don't know what the heck they are. Turn that goofy thing off will you Bill. I swear those thing are great but drive me crazy sometimes." Bill laughs as he takes the phone from Mike and as he is looking into the various apps he looks into the photo gallery.

"Hey Mike did you know that you took a few pictures of that book?"

"Hell I forgot I even did that. Are they clear enough to give to the director?"

"They are as clear as a bell. They have names and amounts, and places, and some notation here looks like EXM and AIC. Looks like you copied at least a half a dozen pages here. What the heck is EXM or AIC mean?"

"Yeh, I couldn't figure those two out either. Could be the initials of some-one high up who was according to the sums receiving a ton of money. Listen Bill do mew a favor, get on the phone and call the F.B.I. director and tell him what we found and tell him we will give him the pictures when we see him in Ocala."

Bill called Tallahassee and spoke to the directors' secretary who told Bill that the director was already in Ocala and would meet them at the F.B.I. office in Ocala.

A couple of hours later they pulled off interstate seventy five at the silver springs exit and headed to downtown Ocala where the F.B.I. office was located. They turned up Pine Street to head one block north to the office. When they got there the F.B.I. director was waiting in the lobby for them. They showed him the pictures on Mike's phone which included some address with one being about thirteen miles south of Ocala. The address in the book south of Ocala once was a bustling air ranch but now catered to mostly winter residents.

"With these pictures I can get a warrant and a team, and we will get to the bottom of this." The director said.

About an hour later, they were in a caravan along side

of the Marion County Sheriffs swat unit that headed south about ten miles and then turned east about three miles. They turned south on county road thirty-five and went a few more miles. They saw the sign that read Air Ranch and turned onto the street. They traveled about two miles when they came to a gate that allowed only the residents in.

As they approached the gate they saw what looked like a Lear Jet taking off to the south. The sheriff's office had contacted someone in the ranch that gave them the code to get in. They wanted to surprise the residents of the address that was listed in the book. The air ranch was a well manicured area with some homes that resembled the Cape Cod style but most of them had some variation of a tower built into the home. It was clear that anybody who lived here was a flying buff and probably owned a plane. Each home was equipped with what appeared to be an oversize garage but in reality was a hanger that the owners could park their private planes in. As they drove along the winding roads heading to the far side of the ranch they noticed several of the residents working on their planes including several vintage world war two types. As they drove along they could see that the air ranch had what appeared to be one long runaway heading north and south. One that could accommodate a large jet if one wanted to. They crossed over the end of the runaway and followed the road around to the home address that they had found in the book. They pulled up to the address and several agents got out of the vans along with several swat team members from the sheriff's office. They quickly took up positions around the house and waited for the director to give them the go ahead.

The house was located on the side of a long grass runaway

and was isolated from the rest of the community homes that were located on the opposite side of the runaway about a quarter of a mile south. It was a big house with a attached hanger that was big enough to house several planes about the size of a Lear jet. The house was designed like a two story cape cod model home with a little tower built on the side probably for the residents if they wanted to go up in it and look over the runway. From there they could keep watch not only over the runaway but the entire area including the entrance gate. The view was such that one could see an approaching plane for miles. They could also see someone pulling into the complex. The air ranch was equipped with electronic lighting. That meant any aircraft approaching at nigh could turn to a radio frequency and turn on the lights. The emergency lights to the runaway were also located at this area, so one could turn the lights on as a plane approached and then quickly shut them off as the plane landed. It afforded a perfect place that was private and secluded from which to run an undercover operation without arousing suspicion. Not only did this provide a great cover area but it also had access to a service road that went out the back way away from the main road.

Just a short distance away from the house was a huge hanger that could house at least a few planes. It was designed so that unless one looked closely one could miss the size of the hanger. The hanger was located in the middle of a dense area and was surrounded by trees that made it almost impossible to spot from the air. Even at ground level it almost blended into the surrounding area.

The swat team approached the building with caution. They went room to room from top to bottom and only after declaring the house clear did Mike and Francis and several other agents enter. They made sure as not to disturb anything so the forensics team could do their job.

"From the things scattered around the floor looks like they left in a hurry." Mike said.

"Yeah it looks like they tried to burn the evidence." said Bill.

"Well the forensics team might be able to salvage something that would help us catch these guys." Francis said.

One of the swat team members came back into the hanger and said

"You've got to see this."

A short distance away and well hidden they had discovered another hanger.

As they entered the hanger, they were astonished to see that the hanger held several jets. The hanger had been built into the brush and camouflaged to look like it was just a wooded area that was overgrown with brush. It even had real brush on the top of the roof, which would have made it invisible to see from the air. There were no markings on the planes and the numbers had been altered and the planes had been painted a camouflaged pattern that would have made it hard to see from the air and also had been painted to resemble military jets. On the side of one of the planes was painted Raven Airlines and along the cockpit was painted some names like one would find on a military jet such as Col. Bill and Capt Rogers. The planes appeared to be well maintained and ready to go at a moment's notice. Mike and Bill opened one of the doors and found several small packages that were dropped and opened. It seems someone had been in a hurry to unload the plane and dropped several of the packages containing a white powder.

"Three guesses as to what that is." said Bill.

"Looks like this was the center of the operation and they were using this as a drop off point to smuggle in loads of cocaine along with some other stuff,"

"Well it's a perfect setup for an operation like this, a private field where you can come and go without anybody questioning you. But what does this have to do with the Lotto deal and how was McArthur involved?"

There were plane chalks on the far side of the hanger where another plane had been parked but had left prior to the team getting there. As they walked over to the area where a plane had been parked, Mike noticed something lying on the floor wedged between the chocks and bent down and picked it up and put it in his pocket.

About that time, another swat team member called them from the far side of the hanger where they had uncovered several secret rooms that had been disguised to look like the outer wall of the hanger and built into the brush so they could not be seen from the outside. There were several rooms including a big television room that not only had a big screen but had several easy chairs that seemed to indicate that at one time or another several people had been holed up there. There were several bedrooms each equipped with its own shower and bath along with a dresser and closet space that would accommodate a person for an extended stay. Even the kitchen was equipped with a cafeteria style line of warmers that looked like it could feed an army. In the back of the kitchen there were several stoves and ovens where it looked like one could feed a group of people for a while. There were two large refrigerators and one had a good size freezer in it. Clearly this appeared to be the central location for whoever was heading up this operation and it was substantial at that.

Mike, Bill and Francis went into another room and found several money wrappers lying around and a money counting machine. Mike picked up one of the wrappers and noticed that it had XEM stamped on it and another had AIC stamped on it. They also found a huge amount of cash. It appeared like there was several hundred thousand dollars that had been abandoned stacked next to a counting machine. Mike said,

"They must have seen us coming from that tower and took off in a hurry. They seemed to not mind leaving a lot of cash behind."

"Wonder why they left that much cash behind and what has all this have to do with you Bill?" asked the director.

"I haven't got a clue director". Bill said.

Mike also noticed that there appeared to be another room off to the side that appeared to be some type of lab. Mike and Bill entered the room and started looking around.

"What are you looking for Mike? He asked Bill.

"Don't know." Said Mike.

"Just hoping to get a clue as to what direction to go in and what this had to do with you."

There were some cabinets in the back and when Mike opened one door he found several micro drill bits, a microscope, some super glue and some cotton swabs. In one corner of the room there was a box of ping pong balls and a small tank of helium.

"Looks like they were running some type of experiments here and left them all in a hurry also." said Bill.

"Yes and I think I know why." said Mike.

"Let's get back to Tallahassee, pick up Belinda and have a farewell dinner Bill." said Mike. Mike called Belinda and asked her to meet him and Bill at Shula's 347 Grill at eight that evening.

"Mike I've seen that look before." Bill said to Mike as they cruised along heading back to Tallahassee. Reminds me of one of those times we had a case together and you figured out but waited till you could prove it to tell me."

"Bill right now it's just a hunch but I'm getting this uneasy feeling that my hunch is becoming reality. I can't tell you just yet because I haven't figured out some of the details but I'm beginning to get a better understanding what this is all about and how big it may be."

Bill kicked back and didn't push it any further knowing that at the right time Mike would let him in on all he knew.

A few hours later Mike and Bill pulled up to the restaurant and got a table and sat down to wait for Belinda.

An hour passed and Mike said to Bill,

"She should have been here forty minutes ago. I think I'll call her and see what happened".

Mike called the cell phone and it rang and rang and finally went to voice mail.

"She only lives a few miles from here Bill let's ride over to her apartment." said Mike. They made the fifteen minute journey in about ten minutes. Mike knocked on the door and when there was no answer. He took out what looks like two small pieces of metal in the shape of an L. down he slowly worked one of the pieces of metal back and forth while holding pressure with the other. After just a few seconds, the lock turned and the door opened.

"Just a little trick I learned from one of my clients." Mike said.

They took out a set of medical gloves and entered the room. Mike and Bill went through the house slowly checking each room. Mike slowly opened the bedroom door and noticed that the drawers to the dressers were left opened and it appeared that someone had packed in a hurry. Mike noticed that in one of the drawers was a case containing dark blue contact lenses. He also noticed in the bottom of the drawer there were several wigs including a short black one. Mike recalled the description given by the police officer who had been hit over the head at the hospital while guarding Bills room. It was beginning to start to make more sense now, Mike thought. Mike opened the nightstand and there at the back of the drawer was the necklace he had seen Belinda wear but without the charm that looked like a bird. He reached into his pocket and pulled out the charm he had picked up from the floor of the hanger and it matched the other charms and the necklace perfectly. They both seemed to be made out of a special color of gold rope. The charm appeared to be that of a raven. They searched the whole place carefully looking for any possible clues that would give them the answer to this mystery, but being careful not to touch anything that would compromise the forensics team. Mike and Bill went through each room carefully. In one of the spare bedrooms Mike said to Bill.

"Bill Am I nuts or does this room seem like it should be bigger than it is?"

"There is something funny about this room but I can't put my finger on it" said Bill.

"It seems to be out of proportion with the rest of the house."

Mike went into one of the bedrooms and looked around.

There was a walk in closet that didn't seem to fit the size of the bedroom. Mike tapped on the walls of the closet and noticed a different sound on one of the walls. He went out to his car and got a tire iron and probed and tapped and finally preyed a part of the panel off to reveal a hidden compartment behind the panel about six feet by three feet. There behind the panel he found several stacks of cash. Some of the cash is in foreign currency, along with several passports and different Identification cards for Belinda. They also find several pistols and a few rifles along with a half a dozen throw away phones.

"Looks like Belinda is more than a waitress." says Mike.

"I wonder who she is connected to," Asks Bill. As they continue to look around.

"There is a book that looks like it fell behind this stack of cash," says Mike.

"Maybe it will give us a clue as to what she was involved in."

"The book appears to be a record of wire transfers to and from Mexico along with some transfers to off shore accounts," says Mike.

"Time to call Francis." says Bill as he reaches a stack of cash to retrieve an identification card with Belinda's picture on it.

"Mike will you take a look at this." says Bill. Mike takes the identification card looks at it and says to Bill

"We better get Francis up here soon and fast."

They put in a call to Francis and then go outside to the car to head back to the hotel to wait for him.

Several hours later Francis arrives and says to Mike

"What's so important that it couldn't wait?" Mike pulls out the identification card with Belinda's picture on it and passes it to Francis.

"No wonder." Says Francis as he looks at the identification card marked C.I.A.

"That's why we couldn't find anything out about her when we checked. Looks like we found our connection to Pete McArthur." says Francis.

"I'll get some of the agents to go over to her place and sit on it."

Francis makes a call and in just a few minutes he receives a call back form one of the agents.

"Mike I need to get over to Belinda's house and I think you should come with me." "Sure." says Mike.

"What happened?"

"Not quite sure yet but let's ride over there."

They head over to Belinda's house and as they arrive they notice an ambulance sitting out in the front. As they pull up the EMT'S are wheeling out a gurney with a body covered by a sheet on it. They go over to the body to pull off the sheet covering the body and the tech says,

"Be prepared, it's not pretty." Mike reaches out and slowly pulls the sheet from the face and shakes his head as he stares at the body that is missing a part of the skull.

"What Happened?" asks Mike.

"Looks like she took a bullet to the back of the head." says the EMT attendant.

"It must have been a pretty big caliber," says Mike.

"There's not much left to identify her. That is her ring and bracelet she was wearing earlier and she was heading for here so I guess an autopsy will be done and conform it."

"Mike do you have any idea who might have done this to Belinda?"

"The same people who she worked for Francis, and I think I know why."

"OK I'll bite Mike why."

"The way I figure it is this Francis. Someone in the central intelligence agency figured out years ago how to get a great deal of cash and hide it from the agency or maybe the head of the agency is part of this, I don't know but I know that someone set up a pretty sophisticated operation that worked well until Bill accidently overheard two of the top operators talking."

"So what did they do and how did they do it Mike?"

"I don't have all the details but with the help of a computer program they were able to wait until after ten o'clock in the evening when the lottery sales shut down, run a program and be able to determine what numbers had not been bought and their sequence and issue tickets to a set of numbers that only they had. To insure that they would be the only winners, they would puncture the balls and fill them up with just the right amount of helium to make their ticket come up. They had all the numbers covered so that after they figured out the correct numbers they needed they would put those numbers into the cage to be drawn out later. They would also fill the other balls with another substance that made them too heavy to get pulled up into the tubes thereby assuring themselves winners.

Now every now and then they would just let somebody win by chance so that there would never be a question on winners. If someone got suspicious, all they had to do is look at the television that would show a winner every now and then. Sometimes they would give some poor slob a couple of thousand dollars to win and a few weeks later they would disappear. Anybody looking for them would just assume they didn't want to be found. In the meantime, they could keep the bulk of the money. That is a clever way to make several cool millions of dollars every year. They were able to do all of this without anybody being able to track them. Hell one time I think they even took in a billion dollars on one drawing. They were smart though they let about thirty people win a million so no one ever questioned it."

"How did they get the correct ones in the cage?" asked Francis.

"Well Pete McArthur was in charge of the total security of everything and it was his responsibility to see that no one tampered with the lottery balls before they were put into the cage so it was easy for him to just select the right combination and place them in the cage when the time got near to the drawing. Then with security watching no one could suspect that anything was wrong. Now because he was so highly trusted no one ever suspected him of any wrongdoing. When they found out that Bill had overheard him talking they decided to take Bill out and they would have succeeded but I arrived on the scene before they could make it happen."

"What about all those numbers that didn't seem to match the lotto amounts?"

"That was another part of Pete's responsibilities. The way

I figured it because he was in charge of the announcements like who won and where the winners came from he was able to announce phony winners. Not only that but I strongly suspect that the amounts were modified to suite those in charge."

"What do you mean by modifying the amounts Mike?"

"As I recall each week an announcement is made as to the estimated amount of the jackpot right?"

"Yes each week as the drawing day gets closer they announce what they feel is the upcoming amount going to the winner."

"Well according to those figures the amount they announced was a lot lower than they actually collected and Pete was in charge of the payoffs so he appeared to manipulate the amounts and just give a portion of it to the winners when their own people didn't win."

"How was Belinda involved in this?" Francis asked.

"Well near as I can figure she was in charge of making sure no one got close enough to the director to find out what was going on. She seems to also have been in charge of taking care of anyone who did."

"Mike, do you know what you are saying? If you're right, this could go all the way to the top of the chain. Hell this might involve even members of Congress or the head of the C.I.A. or?" Francis stopped right there and hesitated to think of where the upcoming investigation would lead him."

"Wonder if we will ever find out the full story/" asks Francis.

"I promise you one day we will." says Mike.

"Maybe, but right now that's for another time." said Mike as he thought of spending the next few days relaxing on his fishing boat in the harbor and having a little cookout on one of those islands that are near the Miami shoreline.

Sitting in the lounge chair on the beach at Crandon Park, watching the sun come up Mike was going over all the details in his mind of what had transpired with the case in Tallahassee and wondering when he might hear from the F.B.I. director. It had been about six weeks now and there was never any mention of anything on the news. Back at the office, Mike leaned back in his easy chair and though it was sad how some people had to get so greedy that they ruined their complete life for the almighty buck.

The sound of the ringing telephone jolted him upright. He picked up the phone and heard "Hey Mike, Francis here, how have you been?"

"Francis I was just thinking of you. So tell me what have you found out and why has there not been anything on the news?"

"You haven't heard anything because we are trying to keep it quiet. Mike this has turned into the biggest scandal to hit the government since Watergate or bigger than the latest going on as we speak. This goes much deeper than we had anticipated. Mike were about to go on another raid at that air ranch in Ocala, would you like to meet me there and I can bring you up to speed on what has transpired?"

"On the way Francis, where do you want to meet at?" asked Mike.

"Just outside of Belleview in one of those small plazas behind the bank is a small diner called the Plaza Lunch. It's cozy and we can talk there and get a good breakfast at the same time." Said Francis.

"See you there in the morning."

Mike hit the hay early and started out the next morning at the early time of one AM. He figured it would take him about five hours to make the trek to Ocala and he was right. He pulled into the small plaza behind the bank in Belleview at six am at the same time Francis was pulling up to the small restaurant. Francis got out of the back along with what appeared to be the sheriff. Mike walked over to the black SUV extended his hand to Francis and said

"Good to see you again Francis."

"You to Mike, I would like to introduce you to Sheriff Bill Douglas."

"Glad to meet you Bill."

Bill Douglas looked like a sheriff should look like. Tall and rugged he gave the appearance he wouldn't stand for any nonsense but would be fair with anyone.

"Let's go inside." The sheriff said.

They walked into the restaurant. It was one of those family restaurants you hear about and were greeted by one of the two ponytail waitresses on duty. They sat down in one of the booths against the wall were they could keep an eye on the doorway. The restaurant wasn't busy yet with the locals but the owner came over and introduced himself and said that he was happy to see the sheriff and his guests. The menu contained several specials and Mike ordered an egg white omelet along with home fries and coffee. The sheriff ordered the short stack of pancakes, and Francis ordered the combination eggs over easy with one pancake. As the waited for their breakfast Mike turned to Francis and said

"So Francis what has happened to bring you back to this neck of the woods?' asked Mike.

"Brace yourself Mike because we did an autopsy on the body we found at Belinda's house. Yes it looked like her but the autopsy showed it to be the body of a woman missing from a local nursing home. Although the body looked like her we got suspicious when we discovered the fingers had been cleared of finger prints. We ran a DNA test and it showed the body to be that of the woman missing from the nursing home. Guess she didn't figure we would check that close but thanks to the sheriff here we got a break. "So what leads you back here to the air ranch?" Mike asked.

"Well when we got in touch with the sheriff he suggested he put a couple of his undercover men at the air ranch. Seems like the county had confiscated one of the homes there a few years ago and were keeping an eye on what was going on out there suspecting a group of residents were smuggling drugs into the county. So we agreed. We then concentrated on whoever Belinda is."

"So what have you discovered?"

"Well she was indeed part of the C.I.A. Mike, but she turned dark about three years ago and was wanted by the agency as a rogue agent. Along with the agency we have rounded up about thirty agents yesterday who were involved in this scheme and they have led us to the air ranch where they claim the operation was still going on."

"I thought we had searched that hanger pretty well the last time we were here Francis?" said Mike.

"We did, but what the sheriff's men have found that on the other side half way down the runaway lives a Cuban builder from Miami."

"Don't tell me Francis a Pedro Gonzalas right?"

"How did you know Mike?"

"If memory serves me right he was suspected of running drugs back a few years ago and although he was set up by the D.E.A. he somehow got off on a technicality."

"You're right Mike but we have had his place under surveillance for the last few years, and we suspect he has been running a meth lab out of there," said the sheriff.

"We have to be careful and aware of any chemical reaction that might cause an explosion."

"Here's the interesting part Mike The C.I.A. believes that Belinda was working for the D.E.A. at that time under another name. In fact we have found the doctor who did the surgery to make her into the Belinda you met right here in Ocala."

"So what's the plan?" asked Mike.

"Let's finish this breakfast and then we head to the air ranch. We have it under observation and all the exits are blocked. Along with the Sheriff's helicopter on standby as well as the Air National guard.

While Francis the sheriff and Mike went inside the air ranch to the surveillance house the group that assembled outside consisting of the sheriff's swat team, the battering ram vehicle, the bomb squad the fire department and several F.B.I. agents waited just around the corner where they couldn't be seen. They were ready to assault the house on command.

"So all of this was just greed that got away from them"? asked Mike.

"Money does funny things to people especially if it is in the millions Mike. Sometimes when one gets a taste for it there never seems to be limit of how much is enough." said Francis.

The sheriff went over to the two undercover detectives who had been observing the house.

"Ok guys what's the situation"?

"Pedro arrived about an hour ago. The female rogue agent named Belinda has been there for two days along with several of what looks like hired guns. We have all the roads blocked in and out of here and we got lucky because the houses on both side of the one under investigation belong to winter residents and they aren't here. We also have the vehicle in place to block the runaway at our command and the sheriff's helicopter is hovering out of site. We are just waiting for your command." said one of the undercover cops.

"OK on my command." said Francis. The word was passed on down to the swat team to get into position along with the battering ram vehicle to get ready to approach the hanger. Everybody tensed up awaiting the word from the F.B.I. director.

"Kaboom" The noise was so loud it shattered all the windows not only in the building they were ready to raid but the safe house and several other homes in the area. Flaming boards went flying everywhere along with glass and pieces of other objects. In a matter of seconds the house was leveled. The blast had knocked several deputies down as well as the two undercover officers who had been standing next to the window. Although they had several cuts from the flying glass, they appeared to otherwise be unhurt.

"What the heck happened"? Francis asked.

There were very little left of the building that had exploded with the furry of a large cache of explosives. As the fire department was busy getting the house fire under control as well as keeping the other houses from catching on fire the sheriff Francis and Mike stood off to the side.

"No one could have survived that blast," said Mike.

"That was one of the largest I explosions I have ever seen." said the sheriff.

"The coroner has retrieved several bodies including what appears to be that of a woman and an older male as well as several other bodies Mike. It will take a few weeks before we can definitely identify those remains but I think this case is closed." Said Francis.

"I hope so," replied Mike as he turned to go

"I hope so."